MOTHERS, SONS, BELOVEDS, AND OTHER STRANGERS

A collection of short stories

Janie Dempsey Watts

Mothers, Sons, Beloveds, and Other Strangers
Janie Dempsey Watts
This is a work of fiction. Names, characters, places, and incidents
are the products of the author's imagination, and any resemblance
to actual persons, living or dead, businesses, companies, organiza-
tions, groups, clubs, events, or locales is entirely coincidental.

Mothers, Sons, Beloveds, and Other Strangers
Janie Dempsey Watts
Library of Congress Control Number 2017901996
Bold Horses Press, Ringgold, Georgia
1.Short Stories—Fiction 2. Anthologies—Literary Fiction 3. Janie
Dempsey Watts—Fiction

ISBN-13:
9780692839270 (Bold Horses Press)

ISBN-10:
0692839275

Also by Janie Dempsey Watts
Return to Taylor's Crossing (2015)
Moon Over Taylor's Ridge (2012)

JANIE DEMPSEY WATTS BIOGRAPHY

 A native of the South, Janie Dempsey Watts studied journalism at the University of California, Berkeley (B.A.) and at the University of Southern California (M.A.) Curiosity may have killed the cat, but in her case led to a writing career.

She writes fiction and non-fiction. Her stories have been published in literary journals, magazines, and anthologies, and two of her short stories were honored by the Faulkner Pirate's Alley Writing Competition as finalist and semi-finalist.

Her debut novel, *Moon Over Taylor's Ridge*, was nominated for Georgia Author of the Year. Her second novel, *Return to Taylor's Crossing*, was honored with a B.R.A.G. (Book Readers Appreciation Group) Medallion, and was first place winner in the Knoxville Writers Guild Novel Competition and third place winner in the Frank Yerby Literary Competition.

Please visit her at: www.janiewatts.com.

Dedicated to my beloved,
Stephen

TABLE OF CONTENTS

INTRODUCTION

Growing up in the South, I was surrounded by a family of story tellers who gathered around after Sunday dinner to spin tales about Cherokees, the Civil War, and our own colorful family. During the Civil War, my great grandmother cried when a band of roving thieves tried to steal her little red bucket. Another tale was about a great uncle who was killed by a lightning bolt while out in a field. Around the supper table, covered with a slick, cool oilcloth, an aunt or uncle would take up the story where my daddy left off, adding something to fuel the story's momentum. As one of the younger members at the table, I sat quietly and listened. I imagined the tears on the little girl's face when she tried to hold onto her red bucket; I saw the bolt of lightning arc from the sky, targeting the tall uncle standing in high grass.

Decades later, with my own children and living in California, I was drawn back to my storytelling roots. This time, I was the one telling the stories and in my own way, with pen and paper. These were not tales handed down by my family. Instead, characters popped up in my imagination demanding to have a voice. The first of these was Maggie, a feisty, elderly lady accustomed to getting what she wants—except for grandchildren. I scrawled out my first draft of "River Run" on white sheets of paper while confined to bed with an illness. I was surprised at how easily the story flowed, of how one "what if?" led to the next.

Other short stories followed, some born out of personal experience and others inspired by travel and people I encountered along the way. Thus, "Erice," set in Sicily and featuring two empty nesters, came about when my family and I wandered through cobblestoned streets of this medieval town and spotted a sign for an interplanetary disaster conference. The odd juxtaposition of ancient and modern made me laugh—and fueled my creativity. When "Erice" was honored as finalist in the Pirates Alley Faulkner Writing Competition, 2004, I was inspired to keep writing.

In 2010, the editors of *Southern Women's Review* graciously offered to publish my short story, "Under Milkweed Leaves." Within the next five years, six more of my short stories were published in *Southern Women's Review*, other literary magazines, and anthologies. One of the stories set in North Georgia, "Moon Ride," was the seed for my second novel, *Return to Taylor's Crossing*.

The stories that follow are not "connected" as is the trend in some collections but rather stand alone. Yet these stories have a common theme. All explore relationships, and feature mothers, sons, daughters, brothers, sisters, beloveds, friends, and strangers. Some are set in the South, others in California, and some in Europe.

As you travel along with these characters, it is my hope that you enjoy the journey.

--Janie Dempsey Watts, 2017

"I have always depended on the kindness of strangers."

— Tennessee Williams

THE SOUTH

Georgia

MOON RIDE: SUMMER 1959

Moonlight spilled through the split in the gingham curtains. Earlier it had been almost, but not quite, hot enough for the cicadas to cease their nightly serenade. After midnight, the heat gave way to a nighttime freshness. A light breeze rippled through the leaves of the crabapple tree just outside the window of the still sleeping girl who lay inside, dreaming of riding her horse.

They were running through the tall fescue, the girl's legs wrapped around the mare's wide body, her rhythm linked to the mare's. In the girl's mind, this forward rolling motion was a circle, or Ferris wheel, of sorts. As they galloped forward, the girl's head rose up to the top of the invisible wheel, then to the front and back down again. She never tired of it, this forward, circular pattern that accompanied the horse's canter.

Alone on her Ferris wheel, the wind blowing against her face, she was high up, safe from the world.

It was a soft blowing noise that finally tempted young Iris off the Ferris wheel of her dreams and away from the cozy, cotton sheeted bed, over to the open window. There, Powder beckoned, her white, fluffy body outlined by silvery light. The girl quietly pushed against the window screen and eased onto the mare's wide back. The air felt cool to Iris, dressed in a paper-thin nightgown, and the heat of her horse felt good against her bare legs. She guided the horse under the crabapple tree, past her daddy's new, red '59 Chevy truck, to the edge of the fenced yard. There, she leaned down low over Powder's neck, unlatched the gate, and headed down the lane.

Not much moonlight reached the windows of Marvelous' cabin where she lived with her father. The cabin was built in a low place where no one else wanted to build, too near to the stream, some thought, and certainly within the hundred-year flood line. Some folks made fun of the cabin. Marvelous and her daddy thought it was perfect. They got to stay there for free, as long as her father worked for the widow woman, Iris's grandmother. Surrounded by trees, cooled by the stream, the cabin, in its low place, was sheltered from the harsher weather and the prying eyes of neigh-bors. On hot nights like this one, near running water in a thick stand of trees, living in the lowest dip of the valley had its advantages. "Any plain fool knows heat rises so we'll have the last laugh," her daddy often said. While the rest of the town sweltered, they were comfortable. Her father's snoring, coming loudly, comfortingly from the next room, was proof enough, if anyone needed it. Lying asleep in her cool sheets, Marvelous stirred when she heard a light tapping sound.

She jumped up and ran to the window, pulled back the old flour sack curtains, and saw the pale, grinning face of her best friend, Iris, motioning her to come outside. Marvelous sneaked through the living room where her father slept, carefully timing her steps to his snores, so loud they would drown out the noise of the ancient, creaking floor. She didn't know what Iris wanted. She was probably up to some mischief, and that's why she liked her. Once outside, Iris offered a hand and pulled Marvelous up on the mare. They would ride double, Iris in front.

"Hang on," Iris instructed, "and don't you let go."

Marvelous did as she was told. At eight, Iris was a whole year older and knew her way with horses. Soon they were off riding in the moonlight, two girls in nightgowns, one white, one black, their giggles trailing along behind.

The harsh glare of the moonlight agitated Gandy as he tossed around in his bed. Working in the fields had its price, he had said more than once. He never seemed to get the dirt off his boots, and his floors felt gritty. Even if he swept the floor, Gandy couldn't seem to get all the grainy stuff off the floors, and certainly not off his feet or out of his bed. He kicked away the scratchy sheets that had taunted his crimson skin all night. Yes, working in the hot sun had its price. He hated these full moons that kept him awake through the long, scorching nights. His house was small and stuffy and not sufficient for a man who worked as hard as he did, he told himself. He needed his sleep. In another few hours he'd be back on the tractor, making a swath with the mower through the tall grass at the farm a few miles up the road. Haying season meant fourteen-hour days.

The white light persisted in torturing him through the cracks around the faded curtains. He swung his size twelve feet off the bed, pulled on some old coveralls stiffened with sweat from the day before, put his bare feet into his boots, and headed for the back door of his sweltering, small brick house. "Hot as a barbeque pit," he muttered.

Riding as one on Powder, the two girls moved through Grandma's field. They were a paddleboat, cutting a wake behind in the silver-green grass. The wind blew in their hair as they cantered along, moving together in an up-and-down rolling movement. It was Marvelous who first began to hum the tune, then to sing the words.

"Bringing in the sheaves, bringing in the sheaves." Her thin, high voice accompanied the thudding of the horse's hooves. Iris joined her.

"Bringing in the sheaves, we shall come rejoic-ing, bringing in the sheaves," they sang together. The mare's hooves rose up through the sea of grass, creat-ing a wide circle through the field.

Sometimes walking helped Gandy sleep. He un-clipped his German shepherds from the rope and sig-naled the dogs to follow as he set out at a fast pace towards the ridge crest. He stood at the top, surveying the sweep of high grass he'd cut for the last two sum-mers but would not be mowing tomorrow. No, widow-woman Tucker had seen fit to hire someone else to take his place, a colored man. As he looked out over the field, the field he would probably never mow again, he reached down, grasped a bunch of tall blades with his stubby, tobacco-stained fingers and yanked up, ripping the plant from the ground, roots and all. He looked up and saw something cutting through the grass and felt a shiver pass over his bare arms as he heard the voices singing, "We shall come rejoicing." He looked up to see a white horse gliding along through the too tall grass not fifty feet away. Two small riders rode the horse, the one in front pale as the moon and the one behind dark as cocoa. He collected his dogs.

"Sic 'em, boys!" he commanded. The shepherds bolted off toward their prey.

The girls were laughing their way through the sec-ond chorus of "Bringing in the Sheaves" when it hap-pened. Sensing danger, the horse spooked and turned abruptly, causing the riders to spin forward like an out-of-control Ferris wheel come loose from its moorings. The twosome tumbled forward through the air and landed all at once in the soft grass, knocking the breath out of both. Powder recovered and bolted away. On the ground, Marvelous still clung to Iris, as she'd been instructed, her arms wrapped tightly around her friend's waist, even though they were lying on their sides on the cool grass. As soon as Iris caught her breath, she spoke.

"You can let go now," she said. Marvelous loosened her hands and sat up and saw nothing but the surrounding wall of grass.

"Where's Powder?" she asked. Before Iris could answer, she heard a nearby rustle and a low growling noise. The girls reached out for one another, grasped hands, and stood up to confront danger together.

The faces of two ugly dogs appeared through the tall grass, less than four feet away. Iris knew those dogs, and knew how mean they were. Almost as mean as their owner, Grandma said, Mr. Gandy, who she had to let go. One of them lunged forward, snarling. There was no point in running—the dogs had outrun and killed a terrier last year.

"Go away," Iris yelled. She flung her fist out in a hitting motion. The largest dog only briefly recoiled, then moved in closer, lowering its huge head. Iris pushed Marvelous behind her, shielded her, preparing for the worst. Her heart beat drummed in her chest, and she wondered if Marvelous could hear it. Then, she felt a vibration underfoot. The pounding of hooves signaled the arrival of Powder. The curs heard it too, looked around, saw nothing until the sharp hooves crashed through the tall grass and landed directly on their rotten heads. The shepherds yelped and cowered and then ran away as quickly as they had appeared.

"Scaredy cats," Iris said. Both girls began to shake and laugh with relief. Powder nodded her head up and down and offered her silky muzzle. Iris stroked the mare and thanked her while Marvelous simply flung her thin arms around the horse's damp chest. After a few minutes had passed, Iris hoisted herself up on the mare's warm back, pulled Marvelous up behind, and set off.

Some distance away, Gandy bent down to examine his shepherds' heads in the moonlight. There appeared to be no permanent damage, and that was a good thing. He would have made widow-woman Tucker pay for it. He shivered as he stared across the field, over the tall grass he should be rightly mowing tomorrow but wasn't. All on account of the coloreds, one of them singing at this moment as pretty as she pleased, and with a white girl. What was the world coming to?

Iris returned Marvelous back home well before the roosters began to stir. By the time Iris made it into her own bed, the cicadas had long ago ceased their night song. A gentle wash of moonlight spilled through her curtains. She closed her eyes and tried not to think of the dogs that had attacked. Instead she imagined running again through the field atop the horse, her friend Marvelous tucked in behind. They would move in a forward motion, like a Ferris wheel, high up on a horse. Together, safe from the world.

Tennessee

RUNAWAY RUBY YACHT: SEPTEMBER 1963

The air outside was hazy and still, an Indian summer day, a quiet calm time before the winter storms blew into east Tennessee. Gentle October heat filtered through the windows of the fifth grade classroom lulling most of the students into complacency, except for one. Toying with her off-kilter ponytail, Sadie daydreamed of her mother.

Snapping high heels on the sidewalk interrupted the silence. Sadie looked out the window and saw a smartly dressed woman carrying a tray of pink-frosted cupcakes into the school. Someone else's mother. Sadie twisted her fingers around stray blonde hairs that sprang wildly from her ponytail and ached for a mother who was utterly normal. A mother who wore a lime green apron and sliced fresh strawberries and whipped fresh cream to pour over homemade short cake. A mother who would drive her to school and pick her up and plait her hair into perfect braids each morning. A mother who had not run away.

Sadie brought her attention back to the classroom and her teacher's gray pin curls. Miss Owens slowly and methodically wrote down long division problems on the chalkboard. Sadie attempted to copy down the problems but instead watched as her pencil tip drew loopy circles across the ruled page of the notebook.

Why were the women in Sadie's family always running away? Even though she was ten, Sadie knew this to be true. Cousin Ruby ran away when her daddy tried to make her work in his grocery store all summer, Aunt Peggy ran off after Uncle John ripped out a hank of her hair, and cousin Darlene ran away after her daddy called her a fairy when he saw her holding hands with another girl. Sadie's big sister Jean hadn't exactly run away, but she had a bad habit of jumping out of the family's moving car when she got angry. And now Sadie's own mama made four, or five if you counted jumping out of a moving car.

Mama first started acting strange, odd for even her, around the time President Kennedy did something to make the Cubans point their missiles right at the Oak Ridge nuclear plant just a couple hours up the road from where Sadie lived with her family. Sadie thought how close they had been to all getting blown up because the school principal herded all the children into the gym bomb shelter filled with plastic bleach bottles containing water and large metal canisters containing horrible-tasting emergency crackers.

Jumpier than usual, Mama heard a news report on the radio about the Cubans and decided to run to town to buy some extra canned goods for the family in case they wound up living in their dark, damp basement while the radiation settled. She threw on an old pair of red slacks with a faded green sweater and beat-up loafers. She topped it all off with her long string of white pearls and her purple beret that clung onto her thin and wild ash blonde hair. Even though most of her clothes were out of style, worn out, and always terribly mismatched, Mama always insisted on wearing pearls with fresh lipstick.

When she backed out her '56 Chevy in a hurry, she hadn't bothered looking in the rear view mirror because, as she said, who knew if there wouldn't be a run-on for green peas or corn down at the grocery store? Their collie, Omar, didn't see her, and she certainly didn't see him. Just after it happened and not knowing yet, Sadie and her big brother Ralph ran out to remind Mama to get ice cream. They collided with her in the doorway.

"Where's the ax? Help me find the ax!" Mama yelled. Confused, but reined into action by the high volume of Mama's voice, Ralph complied and rushed off to the basement. Sadie still didn't know what was going on but figured the next few seconds might be a good time to remind Mama about the ice cream.

"A pint of vanilla or chocolate, or maybe the kind with all three colors," said Sadie. Mama, a free spirit but nevertheless usually an attentive mother, ignored Sadie and grabbed for the ax as soon as Ralph arrived at the top of the basement stairs.

"You all stay in here. Don't come outside," Mama said. Gripping the ax in hand, she started out the door.

"What about the ice cream?" Sadie asked.

Ralph, who at twelve was three years older and somewhat wiser, chased after Mama.

"What are you doing?" he asked, and followed her to the car. Looking through the dirty kitchen window onto the driveway, Sadie saw her mother raise the ax up in the air, saw Ralph reach out and struggle to stop her. Sadie rushed out to join them and immediately saw the problem. Mama had smushed Omar. His middle was all crushed in and blood trickled from his mouth. His wide eyes appealed to Sadie, and he whimpered. Sadie moved forward to touch him. Mama stopped her.

"Go inside. He's suffering. I've got to chop off his head," said Mama.

"Can't we take him to the vet?" Ralph pleaded. Too stunned to speak, Sadie fixed her eyes on Mama's long pearls riding up her sweater front as she hoisted the ax in the air.

"Inside, now," Mama ordered. Ralph grabbed Sadie's hand and dragged her away to the house. As soon as their backs were turned, Sadie heard thumping noises and yelping. Mama was killing poor Omar!

Mama couldn't stand suffering of any sort, she told them after. She hated seeing children or dogs in pain. And since Omar was going to die anyway, she had put him out of his misery. This is how her grandmother killed chickens on the farm, Mama had explained. Sadie thought it cruel and her mother odd at the time, but when she really, really thought about it, it all made sense. Sort of.

Despite being so different, Mama knew how to fix Sadie's hair and how to feed her soup when she was sick and to how to put Vicks Vapo Rub on her chest when she had a cold. In the summers, Mama would steer them to the round metal picnic table in the back yard under the shade of the maple tree. Wearing her pearls, a white blouse and cut-offs, she would pretend to be their waitress, handing out cloth napkins and serving lunch.

"Pimento cheese sandwiches with fresh tomato is our special today. Do you prefer yours cut in squares or triangles?" she'd ask. Ralph and Sadie were expected to say please and thank you and to work on their table manners while Mama recited poetry.

"Here with a little bread beneath the bough, a flask of wine, a book of verse—and thou beside me singing in the wilderness—oh, wilderness were paradise enow!" Mama called it the Ruby Yacht. What an odd name, Sadie thought. Her teacher's raspy voice brought her back to the fifth grade classroom.

"For tonight's homework," said Miss Owens, "you may choose five of the ten problems you've copied down. Any questions?" Sadie had one, though not about math. Where was her mother? She remembered the fight that made Mama run away.

Her family had been staying in her aunt's tightly cramped Washington, D.C. apartment for a few days during their trip to see the capitol. Sadie would soon study American history, so her mother, a card-carrying member of the D.A.R., thought the trip important. The way Sadie remembered it was that her family sat down for dinner after a long day of sightseeing in the hot city. Sadie, her mother, her father, and brother squeezed in around Aunt Tal's Formica table. The air conditioner was broken and the place felt like a furnace. Aunt Tal insisted on making a hot meal. Everyone was trying real hard not to fight like they had the night before when Mama had mentioned wanting to see the D.A.R. headquarters. Tal ridiculed Mama for putting on airs. Daddy jumped in and said let's all just shut up and eat. Even Daddy knew not to argue with Tal, who was a secretary at the F.B.I. and was a very important person. Aunt Tal was always right, and especially when it was her apartment you were staying in.

Tal had just served up some creamy chicken dish with long asparagus spears on the side. Sadie had never seen a piece of asparagus this long. The kind

she usually ate was chopped up and tender and from
a can. She tried to cut the tough spear with the side
of her fork and when she finally got it sliced in half,
her knife scraped hard against the plate causing Aunt
Tal to glare. Sadie focused on her eating and put the
stringy stuff in her mouth and chewed. Not only was
it tough, it tasted awful. A deep, bitter taste, like medi-
cine. She quickly brought her napkin to her mouth and
spit it out while no one was looking, or so she thought.
Suddenly, Tal jumped all over her.

"What do you think you're doing, Miss Priss?" Tal
asked. Sadie didn't want to answer because she knew
any answer would be wrong. Her father prodded her.

"Answer your aunt."

"The asparagus tastes funny," she said. Her aunt
flew into a rage, announcing that it was frozen asparagus, and nothing was wrong with it, and Sadie ought
to know better than waste food. Her mother jumped in
and tried to defend her.

"She's never eaten frozen, only canned," Mama
said. "The Frigidaire won't work if the electricity's
knocked out, so I don't keep frozen food. The way
those Cubans have been acting—well, you get my
drift. Canned goods will survive most anything." You
would have thought Mama had said "communist" not
"canned" from the rage that overtook Tal.

"You spoil the child," she yelled at Mama. "J.D., you
told me yourself she spoils all of your kids. Lets them
lie around all summer reading books. They don't do

their chores, not a one, you said." Mama began twirling her pearls and looked at Dad.

"I said they ought to help her out more, that's all," Daddy answered.

"Excuse me," said Mama and stood up. Tal grabbed Mama's delicate wrist and squeezed hard.

"Don't be rude," said Tal.

"Let go of me!" Mama said. She tried to twist away from Tal's grip but knocked over a glass of sweet tea instead. Amber liquid spilled all over the table and onto the white linoleum floor.

"Stop it, stop it!" said Dad, rising from his chair.

"Look what you've done now!" Tal screamed at Mama. Mama pulled back hard and finally got away from Tal, knocking over a metal folding chair in the process.

"Let Rustum cry to battle as he likes," Mama cried and moved towards the door. Apparently the wrong thing to say. Tal followed her, and clamped her wide fingers on Mama's thin shoulder. Mama broke free and ran out of the sweltering apartment, clutching only her purse and the paper napkin that she had earlier and so carefully placed on her lap. Sadie's heart beat fast during the melee. After, she sat frightened with a lump in her throat staring at the ugly, green half-eaten asparagus. She felt her dinner coming up and got to the bathroom just in time. Buckled over the toilet, she heard Tal speaking to her father.

"Just let her go, J.D. She's crazy, I tell you. The way she killed that dog with the ax. You should have her committed." Then Tal yelled out to Sadie, "Don't you mess up my bathroom, you hear?" Sadie finished getting rid of her dinner, splashed cold water on her face, and returned to the table and listened while Tal, an old maid, tried to tell her Daddy how to handle his high-strung wife.

The fight had ended their vacation. Daddy spent the next few days walking the streets looking for Mama and talking to the police. After a few days, they left for home. They had not seen or heard from Mama since their return to Tennessee. School started. Daddy hired Lottie, a kind dark lady, to do Mama's work and look after the kids. He refused to speak of his missing wife and would not allow any talk of her amongst the children. It was as if Mama had never existed, except to Ralph and Sadie who talked about her in code, calling her "Ruby Yacht." A good listener, Lottie assured Sadie that Mama would "come on back when she done gettin' herself a break." Sadie really liked talking with Lottie, but she didn't like her salty cooking. And she did not serve up lunch with Ruby Yacht poetry or plait Sadie's long blonde hair into braids.

The two months without Mama passed slowly. The leaves would soon fall, and it would get cold. Mama was still missing. All because Sadie had refused to eat her asparagus.

Sadie finished copying her problems and looked around the classroom. Susan Miller was dressed in a lavender sweater and skirt with a matching scarf in her hair. She said her mother bought her matching scarves in every color to wear with every outfit. Sadie's mama had given her and Ralph scarves too, colorful, flimsy rectangles of cloth that she encouraged them to fashion into turbans and costumes to wear as they whirled under the blossoming Mimosa trees. "My little dervishes," Mama had called them.

Mama wasn't boring or calm like the other mothers. With her, everything was exciting but often embarrassing. Maybe, Sadie thought, it was actually better Mama had run away on summer vacation. Maybe everyone would forget about Mama, and Daddy would get a new wife who baked from scratch and wore heels and a fresh apron and looked like the wife on "Father Knows Best." That would be easier. As she thought this, Sadie felt a stab of shame for what even she recognized as not being loyal.

Sadie was brought back to the present by the click clack of heels on the sidewalk. She looked out the window to see a lady wearing pearls and a gray hat over her dirty blonde hair. Mama! Her heart pounded in her chest and her stomach flopped. What was she doing here? When had she come home? Was everything going to go back to the way it had been before? She tried to listen to Miss Owens talk about the fall carnival but could not concentrate. Sadie felt out of control, like bathwater swirling down the drain after the plug was pulled out.

The door opened and the principal said, "Excuse me, Miss Owens. Could I take Sadie down to the office? Her mother's here to take her to the dentist." Dentist? Why did she have to go to the dentist? She hated the dentist. Sadie stood up and gathered her notebook, books, and pale blue cardigan sweater. The other students smiled, probably glad they were not being singled out by the principal, and most certainly not for a trip to the dentist.

When they arrived at the office, her mother looked okay in her gray hat, her not too mismatched skirt and blouse, her pearls, and of course, fresh lipstick. Sadie was so accustomed to Mama's unexpected ways, she simply figured Mama had returned and had gotten right back into the swing of things and was taking care of business.

"Thank you Mr. O'Malley," Mama said, lightly touching her pearls and reaching for Sadie's hand. "Let's go honey. We don't want to be late to get your fillings done." They walked across the street towards a white car Sadie had never seen.

"This isn't our car," she said.

"Hush up," Mama said, hustling her into the front seat. "I got it after I left D.C." Once they were in, and she started up the engine, Mama reached for Sadie's hand.

"I've missed you," she said. Sadie pulled her hand away.

"I don't want to go to the dentist. I don't need any fillings, Mama. I'm hungry. Let's go home, and you can make me a pimento cheese sandwich."

"No," Mama said. "We can't go home."

"I'm not going to the dentist until I eat," Sadie said, placing her arms across her chest and looking out the window, away from her mother. Mama shifted the gears hard.

"Daddy doesn't know I'm back," she said. She pulled a bag from behind the seat and reached for a can of corn and a can opener. "Here." She shoved both into Sadie's lap.

Sadie balanced the can between her knees, opened up the corn lid, and took a sip of the sweet liquid as her mother drove.

"We're not really going to the dentist. We're going to Atlanta," Mama said.

Sadie was relieved, mad, and confused all at the same time. She pushed the lid down into the can and used her fingers to fish out kernels while Mama gaily told her of her plans for their new life in Atlanta. Sadie felt the familiar excitement Mama always stirred up. Being with Mama again was good. And bad.

Mama chattered non-stop about the apartment, the cases of tomato soup, green peas, and corn she stockpiled and the outfits and puppy she would buy for Sadie when she got her first paycheck from her new job.

"Won't I miss Daddy and Ralph and Jean and my friends?" Sadie asked.

"We'll be together, honey, and you'll make lots of wonderful new friends. The apartment complex is filled with kids."

"Why didn't you come back to Aunt Tal's?"

"I don't have to suffer from that kind of treatment, not from Tal or anyone else. Daddy should have stopped her."

Sadie thought of poor Omar.

About an hour south of Chattanooga, they had their first run-in with the police. Neither one of them had noticed the state trooper they passed going sixty-five in a thirty-five zone. Both heard the sirens. Mama looked in the rear view, applied some fresh lipstick, adjusted her pearls, and turned up the radio volume.

"Shouldn't you stop?" asked Sadie.

"Don't hear a thing, do you?" she said, and sped up. They passed through two small towns before Mama finally sighed and pulled over. She gave the officer a huge smile, fiddled with her pearls, and told him she hadn't heard the sirens since Sadie had turned up the radio too loud. The officer responded by writing her a ticket and telling her next time she would get to visit the jail. Mama thanked him, and off they rolled. Five minutes down the road, Mama handed her the ticket and ordered her to tear it up. Sadie ripped the paper into little pieces and let them fall to the floorboard. She felt an uneasy quiver start down in her stomach.

Their apartment was one of many in a rundown complex of two-story brick buildings. Mama took her through the musty, mostly empty rooms, unless you counted the beat-up upholstered armchair that sat in the center of the living room.

"Where's the TV? And my bed?" Sadie asked.

Mama, who was warming up tomato soup in the kitchen, called back, "We'll buy them tomorrow when we go to get you some new clothes."

At supper, Sadie spilled some soup on her white blouse and rattled Mama's nerves. She snapped impatiently and rushed Sadie into a bath. Afterwards, Sadie wrapped herself in one of the many rose towels she had found in the bathroom and called out for Mama to bring her pajamas. Instead, Mama handed over one of her own long nylon nightgowns that swam around Sadie's ankles.

"Do you have a brush?" Sadie asked.

Mama reached in her purse and handed her one. Sadie simply held it in her hand, waiting for Mama to get the tangles out of her hair the way she always did. Instead, Mama led Sadie to the pallet she had made on the carpet that smelled like cat pee.

"That tomato soup ruined your blouse. We'll buy you a new one tomorrow before I register you for school. Time to get some sleep." Mama closed the door and left her in the room alone.

Sadie did not sleep. She sat cross-legged on the pallet and tried to run the brush through her wet hair.

She stared through the window, saw the bare wall next door that did not have a mimosa tree. She missed her brother and father and even her mean big sister. She was hungry, and she would have been happy to eat a dish of Lottie's salty beans. The tomato soup had left her feeling empty.

The next day, Mama did not take them shopping or to register for school. They drove to a bank, a building with white columns. Mama applied fresh lipstick and went inside to talk to the man in charge. When she came back to the car, she climbed in, wrapped her thin fingers around the steering wheel, and sighed.

"Did you get some money?" asked Sadie. "Can we go get my new blouse and a bed?" Mama shook her head no, started up the car, and pulled away.

"The man said that my account was closed. That son-of-a-bee made it so that I can't get any money." Mama's voice had a high-pitched tone, and she seemed frustrated.

Back at the apartment, she opened up several cans and mixed corn and peas into the tomato soup. When Sadic protested that she didn't like it all jumbled together, Mama simply told her she had better be thankful they had something to eat. Sadie shut up and ate. Mama spent the next few hours either looking out the window, as though she expected someone, or rummaging around the apartment searching for spare coins. She found only two quarters and a dime. After Sadie took her bath, Mama came in and told her it was time to go to bed.

"My hair's not dry, and it's still light outside," Sadie protested.

"Keep it down or they'll hear us."

"Who?" Sadie asked, but Mama had already closed the bedroom the door. She heard Mama singing in her off-key voice. Why had Mama told her to be quiet if she was going to sing? Mama was acting strangely, even for Mama, Sadie realized. She lay down on the pallet, shut her eyes, and tried to forget she wasn't at home.

Sometime later, the light was switched on. Sadie felt her mother shaking her shoulder, urging her to wake up. Through the curtain-less window, Sadie could see it was still dark. Mama was dressed in her clothes from yesterday. She heard the edginess in her mother's voice and followed her into the living room.

Mama directed her to the armchair now encircled with many of the rose towels. She led Sadie over the ring of towels and told her to climb into her Uncle John's lap.

"He's not here," said Sadie.

Mama responded by shoving her into the chair. Sadie clung to the wide arms of the chair and felt the quiver in her belly grow to a rumble.

"Aren't you going to be polite to your uncle, young lady? Speak to him," Mama said. Sadie stared at her mother. Was this some new type of game?

With rising voice, Mama spoke again. "Talk to him. You're being disrespectful." She grabbed Sadie's shoulders.

"Hi Uncle John, good to see you," Sadie said. She looked to where she thought his head would be if he were there.

Mama ran into the kitchen and grabbed a broom, and then returned to the living room. Sadie started to climb out of the chair, but Mama pushed her back down.

"I told you to sit there in your uncle's lap. I know they're up there." Mama held the broom by the straw end, pointed the handle upward, and began banging the ceiling in a steady rhythm.

"Who?" asked Sadie. Her mother stopped the thumping and stared at her with wide-open, glassy blue eyes that reminded Sadie of Omar's--after he was run over.

"The communists."

"Aren't we supposed to be quiet?" she asked.

Her mother responded by slamming the butt-end of the broomstick into the ceiling repeatedly. Her pearls flew up and down over her jiggling bosom. Seeing this, Sadie folded herself into the corner of the upholstered chair and tried to be very small and not so noticeable.

Within minutes thumping started from up above. Fear gripped Sadie's stomach. So there was someone up there? Mama threw the broom aside and grabbed two of the rose towels. She put one over Sadie's head and one over her own.

"Shush, they won't see us with these," she said.

Under the towel Sadie quietly wept. Mama did not hear her because she was too busy repeating a familiar verse. "Wake! For the sun behind yon eastern height has chased the session of the stars from night; and to the field of heav'n ascending, strikes the sultan's turret with a shaft of light."

Sadie listened from her place under the rose towel and was somehow comforted by the Ruby Yacht's words.

At dawn, Mama pulled off their towels and told her to dress in yesterday's clothes. Sadie went to the corner of her new room, collected her things from the floor, and dressed in all she found: a slip, the pale blue cardigan sweater, and a skirt. Her mother had washed her underpants, blouse, and socks, but they were still hanging in the bathroom, and were damp. Sadie thought herself odd wearing a cardigan over only a slip. She was even more worried about the rose towels Mama insisted they wear over their heads as they left the apartment at dawn. She hoped the other children wouldn't see her like this.

The streets were slick with a light mist as they walked across the way into a big parking lot ringed with stores. They arrived at a closed dress shop where Mama promptly began banging on the door. Sadie looked through the plate glass window into the vacant store. "Mama, no one's in there," she said.

"Oh, they're there. They don't know that we see them." She grabbed Sadie's fist with her own and forced her to knock, too.

"Open then the door! You know how little while we have to stay, and once departed may return no more." Mama kept chanting and the rain grew stronger. Sadie's knuckles began to hurt from being rammed against the glass. She jerked her hand out of her mother's, pulled the towel off her head, and danced backward and away, into the rain. Mama whirled around, her wide eyes wide open but not seeing.

"You're scaring me," Sadie screamed at her mother. Clutching the towel, she turned around and loped across the parking lot to she knew not where. The apartment building where she'd spent a long and frightening night did not beckon her, nor did the white car where she'd ripped apart the parking ticket. Sadie simply ran. Away.

She heard sirens as two cruisers pulled up on either side of her. A police officer leapt out and ran after her, caught her by the hand.

"Come with me," he said. She hesitated, but when she looked back and saw her mother still banging on the store window, she followed him inside the car out of the rain. She stared out the window and saw two officers grab her mother from either side and drag her away to their patrol car. As Sadie and the officer pulled away, the last thing she saw was her mother sitting in the cruiser with the rose towel over her head. Sadie's stomach twisted, and she longed for her mother as she saw the rose patch on her mother's head grow smaller and smaller.

"Ever ridden in a police car before?" the officer asked.

"No sir," Sadie squeaked from the back seat. "Are you taking us to jail?" She thought about that ticket she'd torn up.

"No, honey. Your mother's going in for questioning, and I'm taking you down to the station. Have you had breakfast yet?" Sadie had been too scared to be hungry, but now she felt her stomach growl.

"No, sir."

"I think some breakfast would make you feel a whole lot better. We'll stop up here at my favorite coffee shop, and I'll buy you whatever you want. Okay?"

"Okay," she said, but felt embarrassed people would see her dressed so oddly with only a slip under a flimsy cardigan. She looked down at her lacy slip and buttoned up the sweater as far as it would go. The fringe of lace slip still showed at the top.

In the coffee shop, she hoisted herself onto the red leatherette stool next to the officer whom everyone seemed to like, especially the waitress. She wore a spotless apron and a little white cap over her thick, shiny hair that was pulled into a neat ponytail. Sadie looked down at the rose towel she was still clutching in her hand and felt a deep sense of shame. She carefully folded the rose towel into a neat square and placed it on her lap.

"What can I get for you, little lady?" the waitress asked.

"A pimento cheese sandwich with fresh tomato, please. Cut in triangles. And an iced tea, thank you." She would remember to take delicate bites and tiny sips when she was served, just as Mama had shown her.

Tennessee

ROTTEN APPLES

From Sarah's perch at the top of the stairs, it sounded like Mama wanted to kill Daddy. Sarah, an uneasy sixteen, stood on the top step eavesdropping on her parents' pre-breakfast fight. Her older sister, Ashley, home from college for the summer, sat next to her, painting her finger nails with fuchsia polish.

"I stayed awake till after midnight, and you still didn't come home," Mama yelled. "J.D., you can't tell me you were working that long!"

"I was putting up stock," Sarah's Daddy yelled back. "We got in a late shipment." Ashley leaned over to whisper in Sarah's ear.

"J.D.'s lying," Ashley whispered. Since she had left home for college, she had started calling their daddy "J.D." "He wouldn't give those kind of details if he was telling the truth." She plunged the brush back into the bottle of nail polish as she spoke. "You can't trust any-one who would throw a wormy apple into a grinder."

"What are you talking about?"

"J.D., your daddy. I saw a fat worm hanging out of the apple, and he threw it right in." Ashley held up the nail polish brush. "That worm was longer than this!"

"I don't believe you."

"Suit yourself," said Ashley. She wiggled the brush in a serpentine fashion, inserted it back into the polish bottle. "They put worms in tequila."

Looking at the brush, Sarah tried to remember the day last summer when the family gathered at their grandmother's farm to make homemade apple cider. Sarah had not seen any worm, and she didn't believe her sister. Their father would not throw a worm in the grinder to make the mash that he would then press into cider for their family to drink. She also was sure he had not done this because her job was handing him the freshly washed apples. Twice, when she accidentally handed him half-rotten apples, he handed them back.

"Throw these across the fence for the cows," he said. "They'll eat anything." She carried the partly rot-ten apples over to the fence where a small herd of cows grazed. Except for a couple of times when she left her father's side to toss the bad apples to the cows, she had stood beside her daddy the whole day, pulping and pressing the juicy apples. Even when the yellow jackets swarmed around the mash and with fear prickling her to move away, Sarah stood close to her father, faithfully handing him the fruit. And where had her sister been during the heat and yellow jackets?

Afraid of getting stung, Ashley had retreated to the utility sink on the back porch to wash out the plastic jugs to hold the sweet and golden juice. How could Ashley say that their father had thrown in a wormy apple when she had not even been there the entire time? Could her father, in the few minutes Sarah had gone to feed the cows, actually have thrown a wormy apple into the press? Was Ashley making this up to appear smarter, wiser? Could their father actually be having an affair?

All she knew for sure was this summer there would be no cider making. Grandma's apple tree had not borne any fruit. Bitter words had replaced last summer's sugary cider.

From below, Daddy's angry voice boomed up the stairwell.

"Work? What would you know about work?" Daddy yelled. "All you do is sit here on your rumpus."

"Rumpus, my foot! I am working to keep your clothes clean, the meals made, and the house picked up. I press your shirts. I write out the bills."

"I'm going to work!" Daddy yelled. The screen door slammed shut after him.

"I'm dead bolting the door at eleven," Mama called after him. "Why don't you tell the whore that?" As soon as the coast was clear, Ashley retreated to the walk-in closet in search of the right sandals. Sarah bolted downstairs to check on their mother. She found her standing at the sink watching Daddy back out his new silver sedan. Mama's delicate fingers clutched the countertop edge. On this sticky morning, the cool ivory tiles appeared to be the only thing Mama could hold on to.

"Mama?"

Mama turned her face toward Sarah. Behind the foggy haze of her eyeglasses, Sarah could see her mother's eyes dampened by tears.

"I'll be alright, honey," she said. "Your father won't be if I can prove he's seeing her." The "her" Mama referred to was her father's bookkeeper who helped him balance the books at his store, and "a whole lot more" according to dirty-minded Ashley. Sarah remembered the conversation from a few weeks earlier.

"Charles and I saw Daddy and Stella coming out of the Read House Hotel," Ashley had reported. "His arm was wrapped around her shoulder." Sarah had been quick to defend her father.

"They were having coffee. Or dinner. There's a restaurant there in the hotel."

"How would you know?"

"I saw it from the bus window on the way home from school," Sarah replied. "Maybe they ate dinner and talked about work stuff. Why do you always think the worst?"

"You are so naïve," Ashley replied, drawing out the last syllable to emphasize the "eve" part. "Why would he have his arm around her?"

"She was cold?"

"It was at least eighty that day," Ashley responded.

"Honey?" said Mama, bringing Sarah's attention back to the warm kitchen. "Aren't you supposed to babysit this morning? Go ahead and get dressed. I'll be fine." Sarah nodded and turned to go back upstairs.

Ashley was slipping her fuchsia toes into a pair of strappy, white sandals.

"What kind of proof do you need, baby sister?"

"I don't know," Sarah answered. "A picture?" Ashley tapped her knuckles lightly against Sarah's head.

"Now you're thinking, ma petite enfant. Charles and I will take a picture, and you'll see I'm right." She grabbed the handle of her white purse and pulled the strap across her shoulder. "Speaking of Charles, he's picking me up, taking me out in his brother's boat."

"Wait," said Sarah. "I don't think that's a good idea." Ashley stopped and faced her sister.

"I know how to swim," she said. "And his brother is driving the boat."

"No," said Sarah. "I mean the picture. Daddy might see you and Charles taking the picture and get mad."

"We'll do it at night, silly," said Ashley. "With a flash or something. Daddy will be so blinded by the light that he won't be able to see anything for a minute. Then we can run away."

"That's mean," said Sarah.

"Seeing another woman behind Mama's back is mean," she retorted. With a flip of her chestnut hair, Ashley headed down the stairs before Sarah could think of anything else to say, which was probably a good thing. Her comments had already complicated things, as they often did. Sometimes words just swarmed out of her mouth and took on a life of their own. She could see the words rising up, a collection of nouns, verbs, and adjectives, unruly words aiming to get her in trouble.

Maybe this time they wouldn't. A photo would prove what she knew. Her father was not a cheater. She would see for herself when she went along with Charles and Ashley to take that picture. Sarah rushed to slip on a tee-shirt, so she could catch up with her sister.

Ashley was standing under the Mimosa tree, fully bloomed in pink, feathery flowers. Her shoulders were thrown back, her face full of controlled expectation as she waited for her date. Like a neighbor's pink lawn ornament, Sarah thought.

"Flamingo," Sarah said. Ashley's head whipped around in annoyance. She tried to wave Sarah away.

"What? Go back inside. I don't want you lurking around—"

"I'll go with you."

"You will not!" Ashley snapped. "Are you crazy?"

"When you take the pictures. I want to be there."
The sound of a roaring engine made both sisters turn their heads toward the street.

"Yes, fine, whatever," said Ashley. "Just get the hell out of here, now!" She waved her hands again, and Sarah jogged across the lawn back to the house. She ducked behind the privet hedge and watched as Ashley waited for Charles to climb out of his loud, tiny red sports car and open the door. From her hidden place, she could see and hear everything but not be seen. The sports car flew away. Sarah remained hidden in the bushes, observing her yard as a stranger might. The grass needed mowing. Some dandelions had grown downy, flyaway tops. She heard the droning of a June bug and remembered the time last summer when her father had run over a nest of bees.

Near the base of the maple tree, she saw the spot in the lawn. Startled from their home in the ground, the swarm had attacked him all at once, leaving his bare arms, neck and face covered with stings. He ran inside to Mama. She handed him a cold beer, dabbed each and every red welt with alcohol, carefully applied a baking soda mixture to draw out the poison. How could he cheat on a wife who treated him so tenderly?

She inhaled the sweet scent of the white hedge blossoms and thought of Corey, a year older and her neighbor. Last week, they had listened to Beatles music at his house. On the way to her front door, he pulled her into the shadows cast by these very privet hedges. He teased his hand up under her tee shirt and cupped her breast, probed her mouth with his tongue. She liked what was going in her mouth, but thought about swatting his hand away from her breast. He fumbled with the clasp on her bra until the slam of a door inside the house caused her to pull away. She knew her mother would not approve of Corey's exploration of her youngest daughter's body.

Tonight they would rendezvous again at the deserted and dark pocket park two streets over. She hoped they would lie under the hedges behind the swings. She wondered if his hands would journey to her southern hemisphere, as he called it. Walking to the park that night, she told him about the plan to take pictures of her father.

"I can go with you," he said.

"Really?"

"Sure." He puffed out his chest. "You may need to have another man around in case something happens."

"Like what?" Sarah shivered as she asked the question.

"I don't know, I'm not sure. I'll protect you," Corey said. He squeezed her hand as he spoke. She felt safe, loved.

At the park, after they flew down the slide, he led her to the place behind the swings, a shadowy grassy area. He pulled her down beside him and kissed her like he had the night before. She waited for his hand to cup her breast, but felt instead his fingers tickling under the hem of her loose, knit shorts. Her body softened to him, and she warmed to his tentative explorations of her southern hemisphere.

Between kisses, he whispered.

"I won't hurt you," he said. "Tell me when you want me to stop." She did not. She liked the way she felt, like she was falling backwards into another world. She found herself not only yielding to his movements but moving towards them. From somewhere far away, she thought she heard a zipping noise. He grabbed her hand and pushed it against his body. All at once she felt something firm push against her flimsy panties. Like a worm entering an apple. She clasped her thighs together and pushed his chest away. He pulled back.

She steered his hands back to her chest, but the mood had been broken. She sensed he was angry.

"I don't like that," she said. "Can't we just do the other?"

"Sure," his voice still raspy and hot. "You're not ready yet."

She had heard about the delicate balance between giving in and staying a technical virgin, or as the girls at school had called it, a "T.V." If you gave in you could get catch diseases, or get pregnant. If you didn't give in, the guy might move on to some other girl. What the other girls had not told her is how good the part before felt. Sarah did not want to sour what they had or lose Corcy to some other girl who was willing. She had heard there were other ways to please a boy. Maybe she would find out what he wanted. She hoped she could keep him interested but not actually do "it" till she left for college. She didn't want to risk getting caught. Her mother would be so disappointed, and her father would probably shoot her—or Corey.

The next evening found them at the pocket park but not alone. Charles and Ashley sat in swings outlining the plan for the photo shoot. Corey and Sarah stood in the sand in front of them, listening. Ashley said she and Charles had googled the whore's—Stella's—address. Figuring that J.D. would not be so dumb as to carry on his affair at his store, the plan was to hide outside Stella's apartment for several nights and see if they could catch their father in a "moment de passion," as Ashley called it.

"This camera is awesome in low light," Charles bragged. "A birthday present from my father."

"That and the toy car?" asked Sarah. Corey laughed. Ashley glared.

"Do we have to take them?" asked Charles.

"She was just kidding, Charles," said Corey. "Lighten up. I like your taste in cars and women." He winked at Ashley, which was just enough to trigger her dictatorial mode.

"Everyone wear dark clothes, soft-soled shoes. We need to be quiet on this mission."

"Ashley, we don't really need four people to catch your old man hooking up," Charles said.

"He's not hooking up," Sarah said. "You'll see." She looked at her sister as she said it. Ashley averted her eyes, and spoke to Charles.

"We talked about this earlier, Charles. Remember what I said?" Charles lowered his eyes.

"Alright," he said. "They better keep out of the way."

"They will," Ashley said. Sarah hated hearing herself and Corey being talked about like they were babies. She wanted to tell Ashley what she really thought. Ashley had an ugly imagination and an even uglier boyfriend. The only reason she liked him was because he was rich. She pressed her lips together to keep the words from escaping.

Rain kept them from the photo mission the next night, and away from the pocket park. She and Corey sat on the front porch swing and listened to the pattering rain, saw glistening and plump raindrops backlit by the street lamp. They kissed a few times, nothing more. Her mother was inside sweeping the bare hardwood floors. Again.

"Your mom sure likes housework," said Corey.

"She likes sweeping," said Sarah, "Not housework. There's a big difference."

"Is there?" he teased. He grabbed her hand and pulled it below his belt, pressed her palm against his pants. "I'll show you big."

"Corey, no!" she cried. She pulled her hand away and slapped his thigh lightly.

The next evening stars dotted a clear sky. With Sarah and Corey squeezed into the back of the tiny car, they headed to the east side of town, near the shopping mall. Ashley and Charles had scouted the area. They pulled into the parking lot of a large, white apartment complex and parked in a space marked "Visitors."

"Don't you think Daddy will see the car?" asked Sarah.

"Duh," said Ashley. "Her apartment is a block down the road."

"Oh," said Sarah. Charles pulled down the front seat, so she could climb out. He offered her his hand. Instead she grabbed the leather-covered hand bar and lifted herself out. He shrugged and went to the trunk to pull out his camera. Using the light from the trunk, he fiddled with some settings.

"Okay," ordered Ashley. "The mission is now in progress. No more talking and that means you, Sarah. Only hand signals, till we get back to the car. Got it?" Corey shot her an okay sign with his fingers. Sarah nodded.

With Charles and Ashley leading, the group trod lightly down a sidewalk bordered by hedges. In single file, they moved through an alley, past several over-flowing garbage bins that smelled like rotting meat. A skeleton of a dog stood by the bin poking his nose in a baby's diaper. She saw Charles pinch his nostrils with his fingers to block out the stink. She wished she could turn back, stop this silly mission. Daddy wouldn't be caught dead in a place like this. They moved forward.

To her right she could see the glowing lights of the Walmart beyond. Inside she knew ordinary girls her age might be trying on bikinis, or laughing as they spritzed perfume on their wrists. What kind of perfume did Stella wear, she wondered?

She looked away from the Walmart. A two-story brick wall loomed in front of her. Suddenly Ashley was waving her hand, pointing at something. A car was parked in the shadows next to a garbage bin. A silver one. Daddy's.

"No!" she started to say. She pressed her lips together tightly and had to thrust her tongue against the roof of her mouth to keep the word from escaping. Instead she let a quiver of sadness pass through her chest. Corey reached back and took her hand, squeezed it.

The rest of it went by fast. Charles and Ashley hid between bushy Leyland Cypress trees in front of Stella's door; she and Corey crouched under some bushes at the edge of the building with the front door in view. All was dark for a time, perhaps an hour or so. Sarah stayed busy trying to wave away mosquitoes but had to be careful not to swat or make noise. Corey kept his eyes trained on the front door.

Suddenly the porch light came on. Voices behind the door. Daddy emerged first. Stella came behind.

From her place in the bushes, Sarah saw the outline of Charles' camera rise in the air, a square, awkward shape that didn't belong in the natural curve of the bushes.

The whore laughed, turned her face up for a kiss. Sarah's father covered her mouth with his lips, lingered. A sudden flash of light made Sarah see too clearly the woman's pale, delicate form molded into her father's embrace. Sarah felt a whirling in her throat. Words tried to fight their way up her throat. Disgusting. Cheater. Shithead. Why? I. Hate. You. She clasped her hand over her mouth, just in time to stop them from escaping.

She felt Corey grab her hand and tug her away. He pulled her along at a run as they fled. Her mind whirled. She could not believe what she had just seen, but she had to. Her father's betrayal was frozen in a bright, clear picture that would not go away.

They piled into the car and sped away. As soon as they turned out of the alley and into traffic on the four-lane road, Charles and Ashley high-fived.

"Now you believe me?" she asked. Sarah could not answer. There were no words. "Charlie, let's go back to your place and upload the photos into your computer. That way we can see them on the big screen." Sarah could think of nothing she would rather see less. She clutched Corey's arm and shook her head "no."

"Can you just drop us off at the park?" he said. "Sarah's not feeling well." Ashley turned and looked back at Sarah.

"Cat got your tongue?" she joked. Sarah simply stared straight ahead. Ashley dug in her purse for something. "It makes you want to throw up, doesn't it? I have some gum. That might help." As though a limp stick of gum could take away the shakiness starting to well up from inside her.

"I can print some eight by tens in color!" Charles said. "Glossy or matte? I've got both."

"Glossy. It will be clearer," said Ashley.

"How many?"

"One is all it'll take," Ashley replied. She and Charles laughed.

Sarah burrowed her head into Corey's shoulder so she could not hear.

When they arrived at the pocket park, Sarah and Corey climbed out of the back seat. Ashley spoke.

"Remember we saw two movies, in case Mama asks," she said. "We don't want her suspecting anything." Why not? Sarah wondered. As soon as she sees the pictures, all hell will break loose.

As soon as Charles and Ashley pulled away, Corey led her over to the lush grass behind the swings. Bushy shadows cloaked the two in darkness. They sat down on the ground, side-by-side. He put his arm around her trembling body, pulled her close.

"We don't have to do anything," he said.

"I know," she answered. Feeling dizzy, she suddenly needed to feel the ground under her. She tilted back, taking him with her. They lay side-by-side with the heat of him against her, the cool ground underneath. She looked up at the stars, saw the familiar shape of the Big Dipper, a surprising sight considering the collapse of her own universe.

She thought about last summer and the cider. Seeing her father with another woman, she now realized anything was possible. Her father could have put a wormy apple in the cider. She hadn't died from it, or even gotten sick. Perhaps, even, the worm had somehow made the cider better. What did it matter? The cider had tasted sweet.

She felt Corey's fingers thread into the gap between the buttons on her blouse.

"You're beautiful," he said. She savored the sound of the words, his touch. His fingertips slipped under her thin panties. She let herself melt into his touch.

"Yes," she whispered. J.D. had done it and so would she.

Tennessee

JOURNEY TO YÂNÛ

O n her third day in the Great Smoky Mountains, it was time for Serena to go home, but she did not want to leave until she saw a bear. Standing in the visitors' center parking lot, Serena planted her flip flops on the hot asphalt by the passenger door and appealed to her older sister, June, over the weathered rooftop of the Jeep.

"Remember that woman we met on the nature trail? What she told us about seeing the mama and baby bear?" asked Serena.

"I don't care about bears. We need to get down the mountain before dark," said June, jangling her car keys for emphasis. She jerked open the door, slid in behind the wheel, pulling her toned legs in last. Serena ducked her head through the open window and continued.

"She couldn't stop crying when she saw the bears. Remember?"

"Probably a nut case," said June. She put the key in the ignition and started the engine. "Get in." Serena eased her ample self onto the car seat and closed the door. She did not put on her seat belt but instead gently placed her hand on June's firm forearm.

"If we leave now we'll have enough time to drive the Cades Cove loop," said Serena. "The woman said she saw the mama and baby bears at dusk."

"We drove the loop yesterday, and there were no bears. Let's go home." June pulled her arm away from her sister's grasp and shifted into reverse. "And get on your belt."

Feeling like five instead of twenty-five, Serena snapped her belt in place. June backed out the car, headed toward the exit. Then the coughing began. Choking, gasping coughs emanated from Serena, a coughing spasm she could not control. She reached into her quilted purse, pulled out her inhaler, sucked in deep, dramatic puffs. June stopped the car at the exit sign and turned to face Serena.

"Oh, I see, so if we don't go look for bears, you'll have an asthma attack?" June said. "Give me a break."

Serena talked between coughs. "The whole point— in coming—was to—see bears—we haven't."

"Your point, not mine. I came to tube in the creek before going back to classes." A horn tooted behind them. June held out her arm and waved the other car around.

"With my allergies—I can't come back—for another year," said Serena. "Molds in the fall, pollens in the spring—"

"Bears hibernating in winter?"

"Exactly," said Serena. She took a deep breath, and continued. "When we see the bear, I'll get a shot for you to post on your wall. You could put it next to the one I took of you floating down the creek in your bikini." Serena paused, waiting for her sister's mind to absorb this bit of information. A year older, June was athletic and pragmatic and not a deep thinker, unless you counted her intense discussions of the Kardashians' behavior. Serena was a softer, rounder person, and as their mother had said, a dreamer with fuzzy edges. Serena had been afraid to ask exactly what that meant. She preferred to think of it as a compliment, in contrast to her sister's sharper edges.

June shifted the car into drive and moved toward the exit and the road sign that pointed one way to Cades Cove and the other way toward home.

"I'll make a deal with you, but only if you can get your asthma under control. I don't want to have to explain to Mom why you choked to death. We'll go straight to Cades Cove and spend exactly one hour looking. Then we'll leave for home."

"But—"

"Take it or leave it. That's the deal."

"Okay, fine," said Serena. June clicked on a Pitbull CD and upped the volume, her signal that she wanted some quiet. Serena settled back in her seat and knew it was best to remain silent. She had won, sort of. Once they got to the cove, a lush valley ringed by mountains, and June caught a glimpse of real bears, she would want to stay longer, Serena was sure of it. June would be impressed by their size and their strength, Serena by their magic.

As the Jeep headed down the highway under a canopy of trees and alongside a cool rushing creek, Serena closed her eyes and remembered a story she had read. Many years ago a Cherokee boy lived in the Smokies with his parents. Every morning he left home to stay all day in the mountains. Although his parents tried to reprimand him, the boy continued to spend most of his time in the mountains, only coming back to the clan after dark. Long brown hair began sprouting out all over his body, and his parents asked him why he preferred the forest, why he would not eat meals at home with them? Food was plentiful in the woods, the boy said, and soon he would leave them to stay there all the time. He convinced his parents to join him. The parents sought advice from the head of their clan and discussed moving to the woods with their son. Holding a council to discuss the situation, clan leaders decided everyone would go to the woods to live where food was plentiful without much work. Clan members fasted for seven days, grew hairier, and set out for the mountains.

There they turned into yânû, or bears. They told hunters not to be afraid to kill them because as yânû, they would live always.

Although she didn't care for the part about fasting, Serena liked the notion of a human turning into a bear and living life as another creature. Forever. Since reading the story, she had been as drawn to bears as they were to honey, although she had never seen one in person.

On the Cades Cove one-way road, the old Jeep puttered past pioneer homes, churches, barns, and farmland. As the road was about to take them through an area of tall oak trees, Serena grabbed June's arm and pointed to cars stopped by the side of the road. People stood by cars aiming their cameras at a grove of trees.

"Bears!" said Serena. She grabbed the camera and started opening the door.

"Wait till I park!" said June. She eased in behind a van. Before she could roll to a complete stop, Serena got out. Huffing and puffing, she walked past the throng of people and squeezed under a barbed wire fence.

"What's she doing?" asked someone in the crowd.

Slowly, and attempting to tread lightly, she walked over to stand underneath a magnificent oak. Looking up into the branches, she saw a dark, bulky form moving at the top. A bear. With the leaves obscuring her view, she could not see it so well. When she moved over to get a better look, her heel wobbled over a small depression in the ground. She moved her foot over slightly until she found firmer footing. And then she smelled it, an earthy, musty, overpowering scent. She saw a face looking down at her from high above.

With his light-colored nose, deep brown eyes and turned-up lips, the bear drew her in with his almost human-looking face. They locked eyes, and in that moment, Serena felt the story about the Cherokee clan turning into bears, yânû, to be true.

A loud buzzing noise swelled up from the ground beneath her. Hot wires of pain stung her bare toes, her fleshy calves. She kicked off her flip flops, lifted her knees up and down in the air, trying to move away from the yellow jacket swarm. She succeeded only at dancing in place. As the venom from hundreds of yellow jackets overcame her, Serena collapsed on the soft dirt under the tree where the insects had built their nest in the ground. Her throat tightened and swelled. She gasped for air.

From what seemed far away, she heard her sister's screams. Using her last bit of energy, she turned her face upward and looked once again into the bear's deep brown eyes. A light breeze rustled through the leaves. A chill swept over her.

Then it happened. She was not scared, and it did not hurt. Transformation took only a moment. She knew it was forever.

Georgia

COMMISERATING

Delores hated it, the wind that blew in the night against the side of her house, causing the bushes to scrape against her bedroom window. The wind buffeted her thoughts around, unsettled her, made her feel so very alone. And she was.

The hedges had gone untrimmed for the past year since her Dewayne had passed away. Actually it had been almost two years, but she always said "last year" because she liked the attention folks gave her as a new widow. It made her feel special, set her apart from other women of "a certain age."

She had first embraced the power of the word "widow" at the meat counter a few weeks after her husband's funeral. Wanting to buy a quarter of a pound of hamburger and not an entire pound, she rang the bell. A butcher rushed out to assist.

"That's the way we package it, Ma'am," he said.

She lowered her voice and leaned over the plastic wrapped roasts and stew meat to put her face closer to his clean shaven, pink cheek.

"My husband, when he was alive, he ate half a pound himself, sometimes more," she confided. "He passed last month. I can't possibly eat more than a few ounces."

The butcher cast his eyes downward, wiped his hands against his blood-stained apron, and spoke. "I'm sorry, Ma'am. Let me see if we have any smaller packs in the back. You wait right here."

She did as she was told and stood sorting through steaks, comparing them for fatty streaks as Dewayne had taught her. Had he liked more fatty streaks or less? Already she was forgetting the details...

"Ma'am, here we go," the butcher spoke. He handed her the smallest package of ground meat she had ever seen. "Just ring the bell anytime you need a smaller quantity. I'll make it up special for you." He stood, waiting for her approval.

"Thank you," she said. As she turned and wheeled her cart away, she could feel his eyes on her, watching her roll away, standing guard as she journeyed to Dairy with her almost empty cart, his eyes protecting her from whatever lay in her path. She liked that. Widows needed protecting.

On the morning after the strong winds, she lay in bed till dawn waiting for the slap of the newspaper on the driveway. Still in her pajamas, she slipped on a jacket and dashed out to retrieve the paper. She was sixty-one and kept moving. If she moved fast enough, she figured death wouldn't catch up to her like it had Dewayne. The office cleaning crew up at the tax firm had found him slumped over his desk after another twelve-hour day.

Back inside, she turned on the coffee maker and settled at the table with the news. With expectation worthy of a child on Christmas morning, she pulled out the "Metro" section, turned to the obituaries, and skimmed the deaths to find visitations within driving distance but not too close.

"Mary Ann Combs Mason. Loving wife of Matthew Mason for twenty-five years. Visitation, Thursday, two to five, Roberts Funeral Home, Calhoun." She quickly did the math. The husband could be from forty-five to fifty-five, perhaps even her age. If the photo had been taken recently, Mary Ann, brunette and with all her teeth, was still young enough to have a good crowd there. From the size of the obituary— a full seven inches in length-- the family had some money. (Why did they charge so much to print the news of someone dying? Hadn't Mary Ann's dying been hard enough on poor Matthew?) She put down the newspaper, grabbed a cup of coffee, opened the refrigerator, and pulled out a tube of chocolate chip cookie dough. She turned the oven to 375 and sliced dough circles.

After placing the cookies-to-be in the hot oven, she moved to her bedroom closet to choose from the

mourning section that took up a third of her ward-
robe. Pants, blazers, skirts, blouses, all in black. She finally settled on a single-breasted jacket with matching
pants, her paisley scarf—black and gray, of course—
and low black heels. She would have to wash her black
knit shell to wear under the jacket. She rushed to the
washer, threw it in. From the laundry room shelf, she
whipped out the wooden box that held shoe polish and
brush. She opened the tin of shoe wax, inhaled the
strong chemical odor of the waxy polish that reminded her of men—of her father, of Dewayne. Using a tattered but clean rag, she buffed long and hard till her
pumps gleamed. In less than six hours she would be
there amongst the mourners, commiserating. Oh joy!

The phone rang. Probably her daughter calling to
check on her. Out of duty.

"Hello?" she said, holding her shoe up in one hand,
examining the shine. "Yes, Mike. I'm fine." It was her
neighbor, Two-Bed Mike. Again. He was a widower who
just didn't know how to give up. She wasn't interested,
even though he "happened" to walk by every afternoon at the precise moment she was getting her mail.
Pulling along his ragamuffin Yorkie, he would act surprised and say, "If you get lonely come on over. I have
two bedrooms, you know." She would smile indulgently
and answer, "One room for you, and one for your dust
mop, there." She never had told him what she felt, how
she preferred the company of anonymous strangers at
funeral homes, people she could feel close to without

commitment. Mourners were so friendly, so free with their hugs. With her twice weekly trips to funeral homes, sometimes more, she didn't need the bother of a real relationship, especially with Two-Bed Mike.

At one fifteen, she slipped her stockinged feet into the newly-polished pumps, checked the knot in her scarf, put the fresh cookies into a small Tupperware container, and snapped on the lid. It was the perfect size to fit in her huge, black purse, her funeral bag.

She climbed into her Camry and headed out. Driving down the interstate, she prepped herself.

"Am so sorry, so sorry, Matthew. I am surprised she never mentioned me. Yes, we were in school together. A long time ago, so very long ago. We were just girls. Your grandson? Why he looks just like you. What lovely eyes. Did she ever tell you about that time we…? Yes, she does look just like herself. Nice dress. Did you pick it? Oh, your daughter did. Yes, of course." One could never be too prepared, and besides, the drive went a little faster during her review of the facts she had learned from the obituary—those long ones were so helpful, so full of details.

Approaching the address, Delores' heartbeat quickened as she glimpsed the Roberts Funeral Home sign on the horizon. Already she could see the parking lot was filling up. She clicked on her blinker, swung her Camry into the driveway, and parked.

After applying a second layer of muted mauve lipstick—tastefully unflashy— she climbed out of her car and moved towards the entrance. A young man gallantly opened the door. She nodded and moved past him, went straight to the guest book. She took her time signing, studied the names. Thankfully, she did not recognize any. She took a memorial brochure from the rack and saw Mary Ann's face for the second time in her life, the first time being in the morning obituary. She liked the way Mary Ann had tilted her head for the photographer. Poor Mary Ann. When she had posed that day, tilted her head to the side, could she have imagined it would end up being the cover of her funeral brochure?

A long line of mourners crowded the hallway leading into Mary Ann's casket. Delores slipped into the line as easy as a snake slithering through summer grass. She pretended to look at the memorial brochure but actually eavesdropped on the couple in front of her.

"Didn't find out till three months ago," said the woman. "And then it was too late."

"Her sister died of the same thing," the man answered. "Or was it her mother?"

"Sister! Just six months ago. Sometimes I think you are getting the all timers. Don't you remember Matt telling us how they used to waterski with the sister? The two of them made quite the pair skiing double. Double mint twins, he called them."

"Of course I remember. Matt said Mary Ann and her sister were the prettiest gals at the university."

"Mary Ann and her sister did always look good in red and black, I'll tell you that," Delores piped up.

The lady of the couple turned to look at Delores, and smiled.

"She sure did. Did you go to college with her?" the woman asked.

"Go, Dawgs!" Delores answered.

The woman held out her hand.

"Sandra Duncan, like Dunkin' Donuts, and this is Rocky, like Rocky Road ice cream." Rocky Road nodded his vanilla-colored head.

"You're making me hungry," Delores said. Sandra laughed. "I'm Delores. Just plain Delores."

"Did you major in education, too?" Sandra asked.

"No, Mary Ann and I took a few classes together. I dropped out. College dropout. That's me." Delores gestured toward a cross covered in red roses with black ribbons. "Beautiful. Red and black. Mary Ann would have loved them." The line moved forward a little, and the two women continued to chat about the flowers as Rocky jangled something in his jacket pocket but otherwise remained silent.

Delores asked Sandra to fill her on who was who—it had been years since she'd seen the family. Sandra leaned over and whispered the names, "Two children. Her daughter, Kara, her son, Nick, and of course Matt." Delores looked at the daughter and son, both of whom had Mary Ann's pert little nose, before letting her gaze rest on the kind and not unpleasant visage of Matthew

Mason. The expression he wore was a familiar one: sadness tinged with relief, the aftermath of terminal cancer she had often seen at visitations.

Four people suddenly left the line to return to the door and greet someone else coming in. All at once she was within six feet of the casket, and then the family. Her heart quickened. She moved into the empty space created by Sandra and Rocky's forward flow. They stopped talking as they neared the family.

Arriving at the steel, powder blue casket, Delores stood for a moment and glanced down at Mary Ann who of course was dressed in a red suit with black fur trim on the collar. From the looseness of the suit, Delores could see Mary Ann had lost a fair amount of weight. Still, with her brunette hair and pixie nose, and hardly a wrinkle, she was a real looker, as Dewayne would have said. Would Mary Ann's husband remove the diamond tennis bracelet from her hand before burying her? Or was it cubic zirconium? Delores heard someone from behind clearing his throat. With studied precision, she gently placed her hand on the casket's ivory silk trim. She looked up to see the daughter watching her. She moved to Kara, reached for her slender and cool hand.

"Kara, I am so sorry. Your mother was such a fine person."

Kara looked puzzled. Before she had a chance to reply, Delores pulled her hand away from the daughter and quickly clasped the son's hand. The men were always so trusting, so grateful to be comforted, especially by a more mature woman. "Nick, I am so sorry. We were friends at college." Nick nodded, and Delores moved in for her hug. She squeezed him hard as though she herself were his mother. She glanced over to see if Kara had noticed, but she was already greeting the next person.

Delores let go of Nick and advanced on to the prize. The widower. "Oh, Matt," she said, cocking her head slightly to the right in a perfect imitation of Mary Ann's perky head. "I am so sorry." She leaned in toward his broad shoulders, wrapped both her arms around the fine weave of the charcoal gray jacket. Italian perhaps? As she squeezed hard, she inhaled the scent of wool mixed with smoke. Pipe smoke? She squeezed even harder. He squeezed back, lingered for a few seconds. She whispered in his ear.

"Are you doing alright?" she asked. The widower answered with a mumble, par for the course at this point, and the signal for her to squeeze again as she continued her super hug. "I'm so glad I could come, Matt." She was about to release him when the dratted Kara interrupted. Why did the daughters have that second sense and always interrupt during the best part? Hug-interruptus.

"Daddy, do you remember Michael Sangler?" Kara asked. "We worked together at the phone company." Matt pulled away from Delores and turned to offer his hand to—Holy Tallulah—it was Two-Bed Mike.

Without the dog and dressed in a dark navy suit, she hardly recognized him. The strong smell of Canoe wafted off him as he spoke to Matt.

"So sorry for your loss. I lost my wife three years ago myself." Matt clasped him on the shoulder.

"Thanks Buddy. It's rough," Matt said. Delores slowly tried to inch away from them towards the kitchen area where she would deliver her cookies. She did not think her neighbor had seen her. She would get lost amongst the food and family, sit down, have some coffee, and perhaps snack on something till he left.

"Dee—excuse me Matt. Is that you, Dee?" Two-Bed Mike called after her. She felt him approach from behind. She continued towards the kitchen, pulling the cookie container out of her purse as she walked. Just as she reached the doorway, she felt a tap on her shoulder. "Dee?" She turned around.

"Mike?"

"What are you doing here?"

"Bringing some cookies. We went to school together."

"College?"

"Yes," she answered. "Do you see any paper plates?"

"Sure." Two-Bed Mike grabbed a paper plate from the large stack that sat among the towering platters of ham, potato salad, and chocolate brownies. "Dee, didn't you go to U.T.? I could swear I've seen your University of Tennessee alumni magazines delivered to your mailbox, you know, when I'm walking my dog."

"You mean when you were lollygagging? Those were for Dewayne." Delores snapped open the Tupperware top and dealt the cookies onto the plate. Two-Bed Mike's hand inched toward the plate.

"May I?" Why he bothered, she did not know. He already had the cookie halfway in his mouth before she could answer.

"Sure."

"If I'd known you were coming, we could have ridden together," he said. "I thought you said you were going to buy cat food."

"I am. After I leave here."

Munching on a cookie, Mike reached for another one. "Wanna cup of coffee?"

Delores shook her head. "I really do need to buy the cat food."

"I don't know why," he said. "UPS just brought you your monthly shipment Monday."

The man was starting to get on her nerves. "Maybe since you know everything about me," Delores continued. "Maybe you can tell me why I'm going to buy more cat food." Mike reached for another cookie.

"I imagine you are trying to find ways to get out of the house," he said. He tore into the second cookie, demolished it with a single bite.

"You might want to leave a few cookies for the family," Delores said.

He motioned to the table in the corner of the room, laden with plate after plate of cookies.

"I think they'll survive, Delores," he said. "Back to you, Delores. Tell me if I'm right, that you enjoy getting out of your house. The empty rooms remind you of Dewayne, don't they? When you sit around there all day, you think of him. He's still in every room in some small way. A book on the shelf, the barbecue tongs in the kitchen drawer, that old leather footstool you can't bear to part with. Some days you even think you see him out of the corner of your eye as he flashes past. Without your husband, you're as lost as a softball in tall weeds."

Delores popped the lid back on her empty Tupperware. "I have to go now. To the pet store, Mike. I'm leaving." She attempted to tuck the plastic container into her purse. She shoved hard, but it wouldn't fit.

"May I?" Mike asked.

"No you may not! I don't need your help!" Determined to make it work, she shoved hard against her purse causing the strap to slip off her shoulder. The purse and everything in it fell to the floor. Two lipsticks, a compact, a hairbrush, a packet of crackers, a packet of Kleenex, and fourteen memorial brochures spilled out onto the gray tiles. She squatted to gather everything up before Two-Bed Mike could check out her personal belongings.

"Let me help." He was already down on one knee and reaching his tanned fingers out to gather the brochures. "Sally Haines, April 5. Ricky Peters, April 3.

Laura Alexander, April 8. Boy, you sure know a lot of dead people, Dee."

"April is the cruelest month," Dee replied. She scooped up the lipsticks and other items.

"Not for those who enjoy going to funeral homes." As he said it, he winked, which made Dee furious. She snatched the stack of memorial brochures from his hand.

"Mind your own business, Mike." They both stood up at the same time.

"A surprising statement coming from you. How could you possibly know all these people?" he asked. Tucking the empty cookie container under her arm and throwing the purse strap over her shoulder, Dee turned to walk away. Away from Two-Bed, snoopy Mike. As she left, she heard his laugh.

Out in the parking lot, safely in her own car, Delores sat behind the wheel composing herself. She had read that a person shouldn't drive when angry. She would not let that blasted Two-Bed Mike make her so mad she'd get in a wreck and wind up in a powder blue coffin herself. She breathed in and out ten times. Two-Bed Mike had no business talking to her that way. He reminded her of a mosquito who just kept buzzing around even after you kept swatting. She heard a tap at her window. She looked up to see Mosquito Mike. She rolled down her window.

"Need some help with that flat tire?"

"What?" she asked. Obviously it was some kind of trick. Just last week she had replaced her tires at Wheels-A-Fire. Mike pointed toward the back of the car.

"Your rear. Tire. Is flat."

God the man was annoying. She reached for the door handle. "If you'll get out of the way, I'll see for myself." He moved to the side, and she got out. Walking to the back, she saw he was right. The deflated rubber lay flat against the asphalt. "I'll call Triple A." Mike was already pulling off his jacket and laying it across the car's hood.

"They take forever. I'll get her done in no time." He said it like he was about to have sex with the tire. She hated that "get her done" expression.

"Do you have a spare?" he asked.

"In the trunk, I think."

"Open her up," he commanded. Why did everything he said sound so nasty? She reached inside the car to the dashboard and pulled on the trunk release.

"If you don't mind, I'll just wait in the car," she said. "I'm cold."

"I can fix that," he said. He pulled his jacket off and draped it around her shoulders. "I need you to hold the lug nuts as I pull them off." Reluctantly, she stood beside him with her hand out waiting for him to give her the greasy lug nuts.

To his credit, he did not talk much as he worked. He focused on the task, and she was grateful. She just wanted to go home. The light was fading, and she really did feel a little chilly, even with his jacket, a navy blue, light wool imbued with his Canoe smell. So '70s. Like Two-Bed Mike. As he lifted off the tire, Rocky and Sandra came up.

"Hey Buddy, need a hand?" Rocky asked.

"Sure," Mike answered. Sandra came over and stood by Delores.

"Aren't we lucky to have our men at times like this?" she asked. Delores didn't want to explain that Mike wasn't her man, only an annoying neighbor. She simply nodded.

"I'm cold. You want to come sit in our car?" Sandra asked, clicking the remote. Delores looked up and saw the lights flash on a white SUV of some type. She followed Sandra.

Sitting side-by-side in the soft leather seats and warmed up by the blowing heater, Sandra talked about Mary Ann.

"They were so happy. Finally, their youngest was out of the house, and they were starting to have time for each other again. Six months later, poof. She's gone."

"It's a shame," Delores said.

"Life is short," Sandra said. And death is longer, Delores thought but did not say. Sandra clicked on the radio. "I'd better shut up before I make us any sadder." The two women listened to the music, a jazzy, piano number.

Delores thought about life being brief, about death being permanent, and about her neighbor. Although annoying, he was alive and well, as anyone could see from the way he worked. He hoisted the bad tire off the ground and into her trunk. He brushed his hands together in a brisk motion. Mike had a lot of life left in him.

He lifted his leg up and propped his foot on her bumper, took out a handkerchief, and wiped something off his shoe, a freshly polished wingtip. Just like Dewayne used to do.

He came over and tapped at her window. "All done," he said. After thanking Sandra, Delores climbed out and followed Mike back to her car. She removed his jacket, handed it back to him.

"Thanks, Mike," she said.

"You're welcome," he said. "I'm starving." He opened the door for her as he talked. She slid in behind the wheel.

"Those funeral spreads just don't seem to fill you up," she confessed.

"You're telling me. I always have to eat a real meal after. Hey, there's a little Italian place down the road. Meatballs to die for."

"I'd rather not, die, that is."

"Me either, come to think about it. Not for a great while, anyway. Maybe we could skip the meatballs, try the pizza?" Delores looked up at her neighbor. His big, tanned hand firm against the smooth, cool metal of her car door, the scent of his aftershave up close. She thought about yet another night microwaving a frozen dinner, dining alone in the dim light of another reality TV show watching young people cavort around and fight among themselves, yet another night listening to those damned untrimmed bushes scrape against the walls. She looked up at her neighbor.

"Pizza? As long as it's not pepperoni," she said.

"Enough salt to choke a horse!"

"Exactly," Delores said. She let him open the door for her.

"Let's blow this popsicle stand. I'll drive since I know where it is. You can leave your car here, and we'll pick it up on the way back." He took his coat off and draped it around her shoulders. She breathed in the scent of Canoe, the aftershave worn by the first boy who had ever kissed her.

"Just a little bite, then I must get home to feed Tinkerbelle," she said.

"And I've got to feed John Wayne," he said. Delores laughed.

"A big name for such a small dog," she said.

"A long story," he said. "I'll tell you over supper." With a light touch of his hand against her back, Mike guided her to his truck.

A pair of teenaged girls walking into the funeral home smiled indulgently. As they passed by, Delores overheard one of the girls say something. It sounded like, "Aren't old couples cute?"

Old? Delores thought. Not tonight, not tonight.

Tennessee

RIVER RUN

T ucked under the warmth of a well-worn, brightly-colored afghan, Maggie contemplated being seventy-five, and her approaching demise. The idea of exiting this life didn't really bother her. As eternity neared, what scared her most was not having a link between her own mortality, and immortality.

If her daughter Charlotte were alive, Maggie would probably already be a grandmother. She looked down at the afghan in her lap, studied its reds, yellows, oranges, and browns. That last summer, 1993 it was, she and Charlotte had knitted the afghan while they chatted and laughed. The afghan had survived her daughter's road trip to hear Nirvana. Charlotte had not.

Seeing the afghan made Maggie feel happy and sad at the same time. She struggled to push the gloomy thoughts out of her head. Memories were like old re-cords—you could keep moving the needle back to re-play the good parts if only you put your mind to it.

Maggie lived in a so-called "assisted care" home which she preferred to call "assisted languishing." Her son Andrew was as cool as Charlotte had been warm. He came twice a month to see her. He had scheduled his visits in his cell phone till 2021, al-though Maggie doubted she would make it that long. She hoped not.

It was unlikely that Andrew would soon provide her a link to immortality. At thirty-five, he was one of the few unmarried, straight men in town according to Maggie's recreational therapist, Tiffany. Like his com-puter and gadgets, Andrew didn't seem to need love. He was scientific to the core, and the only time Maggie had seen him cry was when he was a teenager, and his computer had stopped working. He said he had lost all the information. His frosty blue eyes filled with tears, and his smooth face developed blotchy red patches, prickling at his machine's betrayal. Within seconds, he had pulled his feelings back in and unplugged the computer to take it in for repairs.

"Good afternoon, Mother."

Maggie looked up to see her son standing at the foot of her bed, those blue eyes peeking out from un-der wisps of ash blonde hair. Such a shame that he stayed buried in his computer and cell phone all the time.

He leaned over her, carefully placed his hands on her back in what might have been pre-marked grid positions to give his mother a hug. A "cold fish hug." After taking his usual spot across from her in the hard, metal, folding chair, he gazed out the window. If she did not know any better, Maggie would swear he was counting the proliferating leaves as they blew in the wind. He had always counted things, even as a boy. Did he even notice the many vivid shades of green?

She could play this game too. She stared intently at the afghan's patterns, her eyes following the red squares as they wound their way in a crooked line down the blanket, like a river. A river! What a splendid idea.

"Andrew?" she said.

"Yes, Mother?"

"We're going to town."

"But you haven't left Havenhurst in two years," he replied.

"So?" With this, she shoved her treasured afghan out of the way and reached for her cane. "Help your old lady up, won't you?" Andrew rose and offered his arm. He might not be the warm, cuddly type, but he certainly was a gentleman.

At Maggie's orders, they made their way to the car and drove towards Walmart.

"Why there?" asked Andrew.

Maggie smiled smugly. "Don't you want to grant an old woman her dying wish?"

"You're not dying," Andrew said. His voice trailed off.

"I might be," she laughed as she spoke. If her plan worked, she would be gone after Andrew's next visit.

Andrew would not respond to this illogical statement. Instead he made a mental note to talk to her doctors about Maggie's odd behavior. The doctors would prescribe some pill or another to take care of these annoying outbursts. Science could not stop aging, but it could help control the symptoms.

At the Walmart, on Maggie's command, Andrew outfitted her with a shopping cart and prepared to accompany her down the numerous aisles. Instead, she shoved off alone, a wild look in her eyes. Good. He could check out the latest electronics in peace.

He walked briskly away from his mother and directly into a woman whose vision was obscured by a huge box of Legos. A shower of plastic pieces clattered to the floor. Andrew looked down to see a dark-headed woman collecting 2,426 Lego pieces off the floor. Something about her seemed familiar.

"I'm sorry. Are you hurt?" he asked. She shook her head no. He squatted down and began picking up Legos. Andrew hated messes. When they were done, he offered her a hand and helped her up.

"Thanks," she said and walked away. What a klutz, she thought, a polite klutz.

As Andrew headed towards electronics, he realized why she seemed familiar. She reminded him of

Passionate Patti, a character from "Leisure Suit Larry." During his youth playing video games, he'd spent many nights with Patti. Perhaps it was time to check out Passionate Patti again. He heard rumors that a new version was out. He needed to google this when he got home.

On the other side of the store, Maggie wheeled to sewing notions and picked up a box of straight pins— the kind with the easy-to-see, colored-ball heads. As she pushed the shopping cart, she seemed to draw energy from the movement of the wheels as they glided over the festive, confetti-colored, tiled floors towards seasonal recreational equipment. She picked up a vinyl raft and a "Sir Speedy" air pump and placed them in the cart. After she checked out, she met Andrew.

"I'm going to make the night supervisor's granddaughter a doll, a cloth one," she lied, "with button eyes." As Maggie shared these utterly feminine details, she knew that she had succeeded in pushing him beyond the point of ever caring about the bag's contents, which she preferred to keep secret.

"I wish I had my own grandchild to do for," she continued. "You don't suppose I could knit a cover for your little old cell phone?"

Andrew winced. It was an old debate not worth pursuing. He'd told her a thousand times: relationships were messy and time consuming, and in the long run, not worth the effort. His life was organized just as he wanted. He enjoyed chatting with faceless, invisible people through his keyboard. When he tired of inter-facing, he simply shut them off.

Back at Havenhurst, Andrew gave Maggie another "fish hug" and rushed off. Invigorated by their outing and her new sense of purpose, Maggie fell asleep, dreamed of floating on her back in cool water, a verdant canopy of leaves above.

Upon waking the next day, Maggie called to tell Andrew to bring a blanket and a picnic on his next visit. He agreed.

After hanging up, Andrew tried to call the doctor to report his mother's changed behavior. The doctor was on vacation, he was told, and unless it was an emergency could he call back in two weeks? It wasn't, Andrew decided. He keyed "call Doc" into his calendar.

The morning of the picnic, Maggie woke full of energy. She was fully dressed and in her chair when the aide arrived with her morning medications.

"It's a glorious day," Maggie chirped.

"Yes, indeed," the aide responded. She noted Maggie's improved mood in the chart. Later, Maggie pulled a giant straw bag from the closet and stuffed it with the things she bought at Walmart. She tucked Charlotte's colorful afghan over all, sat in her rocker, and waited.

He arrived at precisely three o'clock as she knew he would, wearing Bermuda shorts and a yellow polo shirt. She smelled the thirty SPF sunscreen he had carefully applied on his face. She knew exactly what he had in the picnic basket—two ham and cheeses on rye, mustard (no mayo), a liter of mineral water, and a bag of barbecue chips.

As they walked to his car, Andrew noticed something different about her. It wasn't her hair. For years she'd worn the same loose, white curls. It wasn't the dress. He had seen it before. Was it the hat? A straw number with a scarf tied under her chin? He glanced at her face as he closed the car door. Then he saw it, a red glow in her cheeks. High blood pressure? He pulled out his phone and keyed in a reminder to ask the doctor.

"Can't you quit playing with that gadget for a minute? Let's get the show on the road," she ordered. He cranked up the car. "Head toward the river," she commanded.

"The park's the other way, Mother."

"Who said anything about a park? We're going to the river." As he turned just past a mini-mart, toward the highway, Andrew muttered.

"What?" Maggie asked. She glanced down at her watch, noting the time.

"I just got the car washed. The river road will be muddy."

"Muddy, shuddy. This could be my last picnic, and all you can worry about is a little bit of mud?" She looked again at her watch. They turned off the highway onto the mucky dirt road paralleling the river.

Andrew groaned as he watched the mud spraying up
on his polished, white hood.

"Over there, pull over." She pointed at some picnic
tables and stole a glance at her watch. Traveling from
the mini-mart to the river bank took exactly seven and
a half minutes according to her Timex.

Mother and son picnicked by the river. He stared at
his dirty car as he took precision bites of the sandwich;
she tore at hers like a hungry sailor. They did not talk.
After eating, she lay down on the blanket to peruse the
clouds.

She was almost content. She chose her words
carefully.

"Andrew, I'm dying for some Pecan Sandies."

"We'll stop and get you some on the way back."

"No, I want to enjoy them here, now. I want this to
be a perfect, last picnic."

"Let's wait till we leave. I've got to get back in time
to work on some code," said Andrew. Maggie rolled
over and propped herself up on one elbow. She might
have been seventeen, not seventy-five.

"I might get mad if I don't have my Pecan Sandies,"
she threatened. "It would only take a few minutes for
you to run back to that little old mini-mart while I rest
here in the sun." Andrew sighed.

"I'll go then, but you should come with me," said
Andrew. He scanned the riverbank. Not a soul in sight.
The air was as placid as the river.

"It's such a bother to haul these old bones up into the car," Maggie said in her best Scarlett O'Hara voice. "I'll continue my cloud watching."

"You stay right here," he said. She nodded. He placed the cane close to her.

Getting the cookies was such a small thing for him to do—and if it would make her less ornery...so much the better. He relished a break from the weighty awkwardness he felt being with her. "I'll be back in ten minutes, Mother."

"Fifteen, I imagine," she laughed.

When Andrew's car was out of sight, Maggie sat up and retrieved the raft from the straw bag. She tried to position the air hose over the valve stem. After some struggling—she never had been very mechanical—she got the dratted thing in. She pumped up and down, using all her strength. Glancing at her watch, she determined there were ten more minutes till he returned. The raft was only half filled with air. Even though it was a cool day, beads of sweat formed at her temple. It was humid by the river's edge. Pumping the raft, she recalled the hundreds of times she had pumped air into her children's bikes and balls. Practicing for today, the big one.

Done at last, she tossed her hat onto the shore, dragged the raft to the river bank, grabbed her purse and the afghan and crawled on. Safely aboard (for the moment) she put her hands into the water and paddled out. The current quickly picked up the raft and took it to the river's middle. She was on her way with two minutes to spare. Joy. Joy. Joy.

At the mini-mart, Andrew searched the aisles for Pecan Sandies. After methodically looking over every brand of cookies four times, he concluded there were no Pecan Sandies in this particular mini-mart. It never occurred to him to ask the clerk. He despised unnecessary face-to-face interaction. It was either sugar cookies or vanilla wafers. Vanilla wafers seemed a safer choice. He picked up the cookies and a computer magazine and headed back to the river. He hoped she wouldn't pitch a fit. The vanilla wafers were proof he had tried.

Maggie lay on her back against the raft's soft rubber skin and enjoyed the sky, the smells, and the feel of the river carrying her gently to her destination. She was in no hurry. She could wait a few more minutes. And if she had a doubt tucked away in the far corner of her mind, she reminded herself: inappropriate or not, action is preferable to languishing.

A little boy fishing on the first bridge saw this: an old dead lady lying under a rainbow coat, like that boy wore in the Bible. She was floating on something. She came closer, headed straight for his hook. Frightened yet entranced, he didn't move an inch. When the hook caught on the rainbow coat, pulling the line and his pole away from him, he screamed and let go. He didn't want any ghost getting him!

The pole splashed into the water, startling Maggie from her reverie. She looked up from the comfort of her little craft to see two slender legs running away.

"Tarnation!" she said to herself. She'd be forced to act now or forget it. People, kids especially, didn't know how to mind their own business. Snagged in the afghan, the child's pole was baggage she didn't need on her journey. She searched quickly through her purse and found the bright-headed straight pins. She pulled one out. Black, of course. Straightening the afghan over her mortal remains one last time, she ran her fingers over the firm, cool skin of the raft. Not unlike a lover, she thought, a lover who carries me to my final destination. She jabbed a hole in the rubber. It hissed back at her, a soothing sound, a perfect accompaniment down the River Styx.

Vanilla wafers in hand, a perplexed Andrew arrived at the picnic site to find only the blanket, his mother's straw hat, and an air pump. The grass seemed flattened in a path that led to the river, and he saw two delicate handprints on the muddy bank. He quickly deduced that his mother had somehow managed to drag a craft of some sort to the river's edge and was (unbelievably) at this moment floating downstream. A look at his phone told him Maggie could be as far as the first bridge by now, possibly almost to the second. He had to stop her. He jumped back in his car and sped off.

Down river, inside her kitchen, Dixie Sikes diced up onions for meat loaf. Her little Roy raced into the kitchen out of breath. "I seen an old, dead lady floatin' down the river," he panted. Dixie wiped her hands on her apron.

"And Santa Claus dropped off a ton of toys on his way to the North Pole," she replied.

"No, Ma, I really did." He tugged at her arms. "The river's high. She's gonna get caught on one of them tree branches and get sucked under." Dixie left her onions and followed him to the car. It was only when they were driving along the gravelly road that led to the second bridge that Dixie shared her thoughts.

"If she's dead, what difference does it make if she gets sucked under?"

"She looks dead," Roy replied, "I'm not sure." Dixie gunned it.

Crickets chirped as a late afternoon mist began to wisp up like smoke from the water. Dusk was nearing. Cool water began to lap over the sides of the sinking raft. Chilled, Maggie tried to pull the afghan around her shoulders, but the fishing hook had snagged a corner, pulled the blanket into the water, and weighed it down. As she tugged on the afghan, Maggie inadvertently achieved a rowing effect, pulling the boat to the right toward a river offshoot.

Concentrating on removing the fishing pole from the afghan, she didn't notice her surroundings until the raft ended up under a low-hanging tree dense with leaves. Feeling something in her hair, she jerked up from her efforts, banged her head on a low branch, and lost consciousness. Her limp head fell back on the raft. The raft's hiss grew louder.

Roy and mother arrived at the second bridge to see Andrew standing there in the twilight, peering upstream, phone in hand.

"Hey, mister," shouted Roy. "You seen a fishin' pole and a dead lady float by?" Andrew glanced up. Before him stood the dirtiest boy he'd ever seen and a dark-headed woman wearing an apron.

"You saw an old lady on the river?" asked Andrew.

"A dead old lady in an inner tube, looked like. She stole my fishin' pole down by the first bridge."

"When?" asked Andrew. "My mother's missing."

"About twenty minutes ago," answered Roy.

"Ten," Dixie chimed in. "The first bridge is six minutes from our house, it takes three minutes to get here, and it took you a minute to tell me about it, Roy."

Excellent logic, Andrew thought. And she looked familiar. He walked closer to better see her.

"I estimate she'll be here in thirteen minutes," Andrew said.

"If she ain't already been sucked under," Roy piped up.

"Roy!" Dixie admonished. "I'm sorry." Dixie studied the man standing in front of her. She knew she had seen him before. He held out his hand.

"I'm Andrew, Andrew Lindsey."

"And I'm the Lego woman, from Walmart. Dixie Sikes." They both smiled at the shared memory of the catastrophe. "And this is my Lego boy, Roy."

As they shook hands, Andrew noticed hers was warmer than most. And what a coincidence, he thought, except that coincidences did not fit into his systematic world.

"Why'd you let your mama go floatin' in that tube?" Roy asked. "Wherever she ends up she better have my pole, or else she can get me a new one."

"Look Roy, you help me find my mother, I'll help you find your pole. I already called 9-1-1, but let's get ready in case she floats by." Dixie and Andrew got their flashlights out of their respective glove boxes and discussed how to proceed, both agreeing that until the sheriff arrived they should stand on either side of the river and try to somehow catch Maggie as she came by. Roy and Dixie crossed over the bridge to the far shore, separated from Andrew by fifty feet of moving water and a thousand cricket voices.

"There's no way she could have gotten past here, is there?" she yelled across the river in the gathering twilight.

"No," shouted Andrew. "She either climbed out earlier, or she'll be here in eight more minutes. If she climbed out earlier we'll need a dozen state troopers to find her because no telling where she is." He saw Dixie wipe her eyes against the bottom of her apron.

She was crying. He normally did not pay attention to such things but found himself touched by this display of emotion for his mother whom Dixie did not know.

"Don't you worry. Mother is tough. Tough and eccentric. This is just another of her schemes."

Dixie nodded. Her nose stuffed up, and tears streamed down her cheeks. She wished she had stopped to wash that onion juice off her hands. She squatted by the water, reached in with both hands, and splashed water on her eyes and face.

Andrew followed her motion with a beam of light and caught a flash of her strong, olive thighs. From this angle he could see she was an earthy-looking creature, even more so than Passionate Patty.

"What are you doing?" he shouted.

"Just washing off a bit," she shouted back.

"Your husband. Won't he be worried?" Andrew shouted. Her laughter traveled across the span of water.

"Hank quit worrying about me when he drove off in his precious T-Bird two years back," Dixie yelled. "Roy misses him." What she did not say was that she missed the child support payments.

Ah, thought Andrew, she has learned what I know: relationships just aren't worth the trouble.

A siren came closer. The county sheriff and some deputies roared up with flashing lights. They climbed out, and the sheriff quickly dispatched the deputies up both sides of the river. The sheriff motioned Andrew to his side.

"Need to ask you and the wife a few questions," said the sheriff. A ripple of pleasure warmed its way up Andrew's abdomen at the word "wife." He didn't correct the sheriff because he was busy trying to identify the sensation—was it something in the barbecue chips he'd eaten with lunch? Dixie walked over the bridge to join them.

"What is an old lady doing out alone on the river?" asked the sheriff. Andrew told the entire story in detail while Dixie listened. The sheriff returned to his car to talk on the radio. Roy, bored with waiting, took off down the river bank to skip stones leaving Dixie and Andrew together staring at the water. Night overtook dusk, leaving gloom to settle over all. Andrew fidgeted with his cell phone, punched in some numbers. Seeing him, Dixie put her hand over his phone and pushed it down, out of sight.

"It's clear she's been lost somewhere along the way. You don't need mathematics to figure that out," said Dixie.

Andrew looked up to see her bare arms, how she shivered in the dampness rising from the river. He took off his sweater (which naturally he had packed, even on a sunny afternoon), and gently placed it over her shoulders.

"They'll find her, Andrew," she reassured him while breathing in his scent, a blend of sweat and something spicy. It had been a long time since she was this close to a man.

"I can't just stand here," said Andrew. "Let's go search ourselves." After some debating back and forth with the sheriff, and leaving Roy to check out the squad car's gadgets, Dixie and Andrew began their search up river.

They walked single-file, calling out Maggie's name. The mud was slick and the bank uneven in places, as revealed by their flashlights' beams. In his well-worn wingtips, Andrew was the first to almost slip. Dixie reached out to stop him but fell off balance herself and slid under him, feet first, into the river's shallow edge. He promptly reached down, grabbed her slender, mud-covered arm and pulled her up.

"You okay?" he asked. She laughed and nodded. Suddenly he was a hero. The way he saw it, without his assistance she would have slid in all the way.

As for Dixie, she thought she had never seen a clumsier human being in her life, except for possibly Chevy Chase in one of his old movies. But rather than being repelled by Andrew's clumsiness, she saw it as an endearing, human quality. She smiled to herself. They walked without talking, accompanied only by the squish squash noise of her wet sneakers.

Upstream a dozen yards, there was a narrow side stream a few inches deep. Maggie lay in the deflated raft perched upon a huge, flat rock situated under a low hanging branch. As the cool river water enveloped the back of her head, Maggie awoke to the sound of her daughter Charlotte calling from far away. Her eyes fluttered open to darkness. A faint beam appeared. The tunnel of light. This was it. She was dying.

"Charlotte?" Maggie whispered, reverently.

"Mother?" But it wasn't Charlotte. It was a man's voice, her son. Maggie was confused. If she was dead, why in the devil was Andrew here? She tried to sit up. Despite her throbbing head, she got herself propped up on her elbows just in time to see the tunnel of light pass her by. She whispered "Charlotte" again at the very same instant Dixie called out "Maggie" in her robust voice. Their voices cancelled out one another. Andrew and Dixie continued their search upstream.

Maggie was now fully awake and mad as the dickens. Not only had her plan not worked, but it seemed she would be left behind in the dark and chilly water. This was unacceptable.

Using all her energy, she climbed out of the deflated raft and crawled up the muddy river bank toward the sound of the voices. She hesitated a moment, looking back at Charlotte's sodden afghan. She continued on empty-handed.

Dixie and Andrew stopped for a moment to decide which way to go. They had reached a fork in the river, either cross over a small stream—another offshoot— or turn back. Andrew was all for turning around, but Dixie wanted to go forward, across the stream. They were debating the merits of each choice when they heard a slap-slap noise in the mud and turned around to see a wraithlike figure in the rising mist.

"Mother?" Andrew ran to his mother's side and put an arm around her shoulder.

"You manage to get the Pecan Sandies?"

"Vanilla Wafers," he said. Maggie almost made a rude comment about his choice but held her tongue. Dixie took Andrew's sweater from her own shoulders and gently placed it around Maggie's.

"I thought I'd have myself a little ride down the river," said Maggie. And kill myself, she didn't say. It would never do to tell her son what she was really planning.

"Mother's quite the adventurer," Andrew explained.

"Thought you never noticed," said Maggie matter-of-factly. "Anyway, the raft sprung a leak and sank over there."

"Did you see a fishing pole?" asked Dixie.

"Derned thing got me off course. It snagged Charlotte's afghan, ended up pulling me into that guppy pool." Maggie stopped, looked back at the drowning afghan. "Andrew, go get it, won't you?"

"We need to get you into some dry clothes, Mother. We'll get it later," Andrew said.

"Go ahead, Andrew. Roy will go crazy if we don't get his pole back," Dixie appealed to him. At the sound of her voice, Andrew trotted off.

"Does Andrew know you?" asked Maggie. Maggie didn't know who this woman was, but she was starting to like her already.

"We met by accident," answered Dixie. "Twice."

"What a coincidence!" Maggie said, yet she knew it was not. Unlike Andrew, she was a firm believer in fate. Dixie drew closer to Maggie.

"I had an afghan once," said Dixie. "It was the prettiest thing—all shades of blue. My Grandma made it for me. Moths got into it—must have fed an army. I didn't care. I loved that old afghan. Then, when I was on my honeymoon, Mama tossed it out."

"You're married?" asked Maggie.

"Not anymore."

"Good," said Maggie.

Dixie thought it an odd reply, but Andrew had mentioned his mother was eccentric. They both looked up to see Andrew walking clumsily toward them under the weight of the heavy, wet afghan with the pole sticking out like a single antenna. Maggie and Dixie laughed together.

"We'll take your afghan back to my house, get you both dried out," said Dixie, "make some hot coffee."

"Decaf. We can't stay too long," said Maggie, testing the waters. "Andrew, has to get back and play on his computer."

"It can wait, Mother," he replied.

Maggie had never known her son to miss any computer-related activity for any reason whatsoever. She grinned. In the dark, no one saw. They continued along the river toward the second bridge. Maggie stared at the black water. Just an ordinary old river, not the River Styx, not for me, she thought.

As they approached the bridge, Andrew pointed up his light to see Roy wildly waving his arms.

In the growing darkness, the boy and the bridge appeared as one to Maggie. Her river run hadn't turned out as she'd intended, yet her journey had brought her to this place. And as any plain fool could see, the bridge was more than just a span over the river. For her, it was a link back to life.

Tennessee

AUNT TRISH'S WEDDING GIFT

I saved Aunt Trish's gift for last. Like my aunt, her gift was the heaviest, the loudest, and could not be ignored. For my last birthday, she had given me a jar filled with June bugs, and her anniversary gift to my parents was a garden hose which reminded her of the couple, she said. Not the kinky kind.

"Come on, Sally!" she ordered. She was wearing a brightly-flowered tunic and what appeared to be purple, polka-dotted flannel pajama pants, an outfit that looked like it was left over either from her most recent Caribbean cruise or last night's slumber party.

With some apprehension, I rose from my chair and walked to the bulky gift, wrapped in lime green tissue and placed smack dab in the middle of the ring of chairs where my guests were seated.

"And this one, as you may have guessed, is from my Aunt Trish," I said as I read the gift card which was covered with faux white fur. "Shagadelic, baby! A special gift for you, and John. Love, Aunt Trish. Thank you, Aunt Trish." I ripped off the tissue on the top revealing a giant white bowl of sorts. "Oh, it's white, it's a—"

"Feeding dish for a Great Dane?" someone shouted. Giggles filled the room. I rushed to pull off the rest of the paper, only to see a toilet bowl. Everyone laughed. I wasn't sure what to say.

"Oh my! How original. Thank you, Aunt Trish. I think the apartment already has toilets," I said. "But we can keep it as a spare."

"You silly gal," Aunt Trish said. "Look there in the bottom." I bent down over the toilet bowl, and with some hesitation, put my hand down into the canal, a place I'd only explored before with a toilet brush. Everyone clapped and cheered me on. My fingers felt a rectangular packet. I pulled it up. A packet of zucchini seeds. The women cackled. Aunt Trish continued, "You can plant them seeds and see what comes up, if you know what I mean." She threw her head back and snorted. I blushed.

"Alright, I'll do that Trish. Thank you. Anyone want some more quiche? What about another sweet tea, anyone?" No one answered. They had all stood up to take cell phone photos of the toilet and Aunt Trish.

My sister motioned me over. "Sally, get over here so we can get a shot of you with our aunt and the —" she laughed as she tried to finish her sentence.

"Zucchinis," another friend shouted out. "Her zucchinis."

"John's zucchinis," someone else yelled. Everyone howled except me. I had tried to plan a classy event, but Mama insisted I invite her sister. Once again, Aunt Trish had taken over with her outlandishness.

Ever the good sport, I walked over and grabbed the packet of seeds and held it up in the air while kneeling next to the toilet. "Me and my zucchinis, folks." I smiled while everyone snapped. Aunt Trish stood next to me, beaming. I was saved by Mama calling from the dining room.

"The chocolate lava cakes are done. And coffee." My friends abandoned the photo session and followed Mama and the smell of coffee and chocolate. I was about to walk away too, but Aunt Trish reached out for my arm and stopped me.

"I've got some potting soil in the car," she said. "Now don't you let me forget it. You can plant them when you get home from the honeymoon. If things don't work out, you'll still have John's zucchinis." She snickered at her own joke. I just shook my head and walked away to join the others. I didn't want to tell her what I really thought—she was full of it. And herself.

After the shower fiasco, I made Mama personally promise to have someone babysit my aunt during the entire wedding. To her credit, Mama kept Aunt Trish on a tight leash. Mama told Trish that she needed help watching one of our cousins who had been convicted of shoplifting. "Your job is to follow her around and make sure she keeps out of everyone's handbags." Given a task, Aunt Trish knew how to follow through. She talked cousin Millie's ear off because as everyone knew, Trish could talk the ears off a brass billy goat. Millie didn't have a moment to spare she was so busy answering all of Trish's questions. What color was that hair dye? How much did she pay for those shoes? Where did she buy her dress? What kind of face cream did she use? Had the change affected her love life? And most importantly, who did her spraying for termites?

After our honeymoon, John and I arrived at our two-bedroom apartment and were surprised to find the toilet on our patio filled with dirt and apparently with already-planted seeds. We found Aunt Trish's note attached to the toilet bowl. It said, "Water three times a week, with water, not the other, John." John laughed. I did not.

A couple of weeks later, the seedlings came up. Begrudgingly, I watered them, but not so much because I cared; I just couldn't stand to see them die. John and I would sit on the porch and drink a glass of wine after work, and I'd glance over at the plants which seemed to be growing without much tending.

One night we invited another couple over for drinks before we all went out to dinner. John's co-worker,

Sophia, and her scruffy looking boyfriend, Richard, were halfway through a second glass of Pinot Grigio when we wandered onto the patio. She pointed to the toilet bowl.

"Oh, Sally," she said. "A potty. How cute." Then she turned to John, "I thought you said your wife was sophisticated."

"Sally is, but her aunt isn't," John said. "She gave us the toilet. She's as large as a hippo and the black sheep of the family." Sophia reached out and touched John's arm with her svelte fingers.

"How can she be a hippo and a sheep?" she asked. "Sometimes you say the silliest things. Like last week at Franco's when you told the waiter it was our anniversary, so we'd get the free tiramisu."

John laughed, and added, "That's not the way I remember it." He glanced over at me. I mouthed the words, "Free tiramisu?" John shrugged and picked up the wine bottle to pour her another glass of wine.

After a dinner where Sophia flirted non-stop with John, making her boyfriend and me uncomfortable, it was time to say goodbye. When the valet brought up their car, Sophia wobbled over to John and gripped him in a long embrace. When she finally let him go, she turned to me and waved her slim tentacles, "Bye, bye hippo girl." Not looking at each other, John and I climbed into our car and headed home.

"Why did you call my aunt a hippo?" I asked. He shifted into second.

"She is rather large, in case you haven't noticed."

"And when did you and Sophia go to lunch?" I asked. He sighed.

"Last week, and she was the one who told the waiter it was our anniversary."

"Did you tell the waiter you were married to someone else?"

"I let it pass. It was a joke. Are you going to get all jealous on me now? You go out to lunch all the time with your co-workers."

"They are women, and a few men. And none of them, not a one, ever said they were married to me, even as a joke."

"Well, the women wouldn't, that's for sure."

"What? Are you trying to change the subject here?"

"So what if I am? You're acting insecure, Sally. We went to lunch—it's not like I slept with her." He whipped the car around a corner, and I shifted in my seat.

"Whoa. Could you slow down a bit?"

"You want to drive?" He slammed on the brakes, handed me the key and jumped out of the car. "Because I don't want to be with you right now." As I watched him walk away, I sat there for a moment trying to figure out what was going on. Apparently a lot.

Back at home, I arrived to an empty house. He had not made it home and hadn't called. I walked onto the patio and looked out toward the street. No sign of him, even though it was after midnight. I looked down at the toilet bowl and kicked it with the point of my heel before going inside to undress. I hated Aunt Trish's wedding gift, I despised Sophia, and I found John's behavior puzzling.

After a few fitful hours lying in bed and waiting to hear him come home, I stirred just before dawn to the sound of a key in the lock. I jumped up and peeked through a crack in the door. With his shirt tail out and his hair tousled, John entered the living room and headed for the kitchen. He turned on the faucet and got a glass of water before going to lie down on the couch. At least he was safe. I fell asleep.

When I awoke a few hours later, he was already gone. I saw a note on the kitchen counter. The note said, "You're no fun anymore. I'll be staying at my brother's tonight." I walked out to the patio and sat down in the lawn chair next to those stubborn zucchini plants raising their leafy heads towards the new day. I read John's words again. So I was "no fun"? I looked at the toilet and thought of Aunt Trish.

Despite her rough edges, even she had a sense of humor. She had enjoyed a long and happy marriage with her husband until he passed on. I thought of Uncle Joe and his talking fish he brought to every family reunion, of the way Aunt Trish always threw her head back and laughed at his same old gags as though they were new every time. Maybe Aunt Trish was wiser than I thought.

After work, I stopped off at a little costume shop a few blocks away to try on some outfits. I found the perfect one, considering the situation. I signed the rental agreement, gave the clerk my credit card, and left the store wearing my costume. Trying to parallel park wearing an animal head was hard, but I did it. Somewhat awkwardly, I walked up the flight of stairs to John's brother's place. I knocked on the door and waited. After a minute or so, the door opened. It was my husband.

His mouth dropped open when he saw me—a pink hippo standing at the door. Through the mask I spoke. I know my words must have sounded muffled. "I forgot to bring the tiramisu."

"Sally?"

"It's me, I'm ready to have some fun." He reached out and plucked the huge mask off my head and set it aside.

"I was a jackass, wasn't I?" he said.

I nodded. "You were."

"I'm sorry," he said. "I'm going to steer clear of Sophia from now on." He reached out and wrapped his arms around my pink furry shoulders. "That costume is all wrong on you. You're more of a fox." He kissed me on my cheek. "Let's go home." He took my paw. "I hate being away from you." We headed to the car. He opened the passenger door for me, and I climbed in. He handed me my tail and went back to retrieve my head.

Back at home, when I was about to take off my hippo costume, John came over and whispered in my ear. "Maybe you should leave it on, you beast."

"You think?" I laughed. He responded by squeezing my pink furry tail.

CALIFORNIA

California

CLANFUSION

I t was 4:15 the afternoon of our wedding rehearsal. The entire wedding party, minus my older sister and bridesmaid, stood waiting in the crowded church vestibule. As the priest glanced at his watch, tensions ran high. I looked around at the restless group and realized we were lined up like opposing football teams waiting for kickoff. My groom's team lined up on one side, mine on the other. We were ready to play, but where was Ivy?

My team included Rita, my thin, exotic older sister, and Mama, calm and collected, secure in the knowledge she was finally marrying off her youngest daughter. My maid of honor and best friend, Eve, framed by her honey-colored, thick mane, gave me a reassuring smile. I smiled back. Our third grade teacher had dubbed us the "Gold Dust Twins" because of our blonde locks, one of which I now nervously twisted around my forefinger as I peered at the doorway, willing my tardy sister to arrive.

Our opposing team was headed by my betrothed, Robert, lined up next to his family, a PG version of *The Godfather*. All were all dark, intense, and punctual. His mother and aunt fretted and whispered, but their voices echoed in the tight space. I could barely make out the words "Ivy" and "how rude." I cringed and wondered if it were possible to sink through the cool, red-tiled floor. The uncle and my future father-in-law talked baseball scores while my husband's slightly pudgy, teenaged cousin, Anthony, made small talk with the priest. Robert looked up at me with his warm brown eyes and uttered not a word: it was all in his look. Where is your sister? His eyes shifted as he peered towards his family, then back again at me. Why couldn't Ivy have been on time?

"Perhaps we should start without her?" the priest tactfully suggested. Robert's Aunt Lucy answered for all of us.

"Yes, let's go ahead," Lucy said. "We can't wait around for Ivy." I wondered when she had been named head of this event. All of his family chimed in, "Yes, let's go ahead." Robert looked over at me, and I shrugged. What choice did I have anyway? Aunt Lucy had made her ruling. And for the sake of family harmony, my new family, I thought, I'd go along.

The priest lined up everyone and began walking us through our paces. The wedding coordinator instructed Rita on the proper walk, slow, unrushed, with a slight pause after each step. Rita was half-way down the aisle when the vestibule door creaked open.

"Hi, sorry I'm late. I lost the key to the car and had to call Triple A," Ivy explained. Out of the corner of my eye, I caught a glance of Aunt Lucy rolling her eyes. "Where do you want me to stand?" Ivy addressed the coordinator, who ushered her to the end of the aisle.

Snug in her size eighteen designer jeans, my sister Ivy was larger than life. She held two advanced degrees, drove a Bentley Continental, and had jetted around the world with her former husband. She was boisterous and outspoken, and you always knew where she stood on any subject. She had made as many enemies along the way as she had friends. She was like the color orange—you either liked it or you didn't. I had lectured her extensively before the rehearsal to "tone it down," and as she stood at the end of the aisle, awaiting her cue, she appeared unusually cooperative for someone who was suspicious of her little sister marrying into the Catholic faith.

The rehearsal went smoothly, to a point. We were at the altar, about to recess when the priest explained how we would pair off: ushers would escort bridesmaids according to height. Rita would recess with my future father-in-law, Franco, Ivy with Anthony, and Eve with Uncle Paul, Lucy's husband. Father Rick explained this to us as giggles started from down the line toward

Ivy's end. Her muffled voice reverberated throughout the cavernous, empty sanctuary as she spoke to Rita.

"Why do I have to walk with the fat one?" Ivy asked Rita. I could hear Rita trying to shut her up, but Ivy just giggled in response. Once again, I wondered about the physics of sinking through the clay tiles, away from this moment of pure, crystallized embarrassment.

We exited past the family, into the late afternoon sun, famished and happy to be going to dinner. Robert reached out for my hand, and we were about to climb into our Volvo to head for the restaurant when I heard Lucy's whiney voice.

"Robert, could you ride with us? Uncle Paul doesn't know the way." Robert squeezed my hand and departed for his family's rented mini-van. I got into our car alone, since the others had already left. Ivy insisted that Rita, Eve, and Mama had to experience the purr of her Bentley engine. I drove along slowly, feeling sorry for myself, wondering if this were the way my marriage would be. Unending compromises.

The child of divorced parents, the sister of a divorcee, I was ambivalent about marriage until one brisk November afternoon on the beach. Robert ran ahead of me, jumped up and down in the waves, then bent over for something. He ran back to me cradling something in his hands. Like a little boy with a seashell, I thought.

"What do you think it is?" he teased. He knew how curious I was. I tried to pry his hands open, but he took off running. I pumped my long legs into action and took off after him. I finally caught up about a quarter of mile later when he tripped, or pretended to, and landed in a heap on the sand. I jumped on top of him, and dove for his clasped hands. He slowly unfolded them, revealing a sea-blue aquamarine ring in a platinum setting.

"It's not traditional for an engagement ring, but it reminds me of your eyes," he said. His tender, almond gaze melted me. "Well?'

"Yes," I said. The sea roared behind me, affirmed my answer. He slipped the ring on my finger and pulled me down on top of his chest into a bear hug. We both laughed and rolled over, frolicked in the sand. I had never felt so sure of anything in all my life.

Now, on the eve before my wedding day, doubt began a low cackle in my mind, threatening the perfect certainty I felt on the beach that day. The last to arrive at the seaside restaurant, I was led into the cool, dark space by a busty mermaid hostess. The booths were done up as giant seashells, with tabletops the delicate pink of a shell's interior while the wall was a gargantuan mural of Neptune surrounded by mermaids. A heavy fish smell, mixed with the occasional ocean breeze wafting through open windows, hung in the air. Robert's family, harboring memories of Atlantic City, and picking up the tab for this night, had insisted on a seafood restaurant. I hated fish.

The hostess led me to a corner where my groom and his family were already huddled in a huge seashell booth, menus in hand. As I came up, they fell into silence.

"Hey," I said as I passed. "Can't we all sit together?" Aunt Lucy answered for the group.

"There wasn't any table large enough for us," she said. "This was the best we could do." All of their grim faces tilted up at me. I'd seen happier groups at funerals.

"Well," Ivy whispered to me as I arrived at my family's booth, "so much for the bonding idea that lies beneath every good rehearsal dinner." Whenever possible, Ivy liked to show off her vast wealth of knowledge on every subject. Robert excused himself from his group, came over to sit beside me while Mama, Ivy, Rita, and Eve pored over the menu choices. I leaned in close to him.

"What's up with your family? They look like someone just died. Is something wrong?" Instead of answering, he focused on the waiter, now pouring red wine in everyone's glasses. Who had ordered red? I only drank rosé. "Did you hear me?" I asked. At this point, a normal person might have dropped it, but not me. Driven by my insatiable curiosity, I had to know what was going on here?

"Robert?" I reached out to touch his hand under the table to make my point. He pulled his hand away and seethed under his breath.

"Your sister," he started to say.

"She told us she locked herself out of the car. I mean, can't they get over it?"

"Would you be quiet and let me finish?" he snapped. I grabbed my wine glass, took a sip of the musty red, and steeled myself. I felt a fight brewing in the salty evening air.

"Your sister made a rude comment and Aunt Lucy overheard," he whispered.

"What else is new?" I replied, quickly realizing it was the wrong thing to say.

His eyes seemed to grow darker. "She said she didn't want to walk with the fat one, my cousin, Anthony. Aunt Lucy is very sensitive about her son's weight," he whispered.

Oh no, I thought, but quickly defended Ivy. "She was joking. Obviously. Like she has room to talk." We both looked at my sister, now stuffing wads of bread into her mouth and gulping wine like a sailor. Mama, sitting next to her, looked positively elegant as she tore a tiny, neat piece of bread and delicately applied butter. I knew deep down that Ivy's behavior often embarrassed Mama, yet she kept quiet in order to keep the peace. Mama never corrected her children in public. I was sure when they were alone later, Mama would quietly remind Ivy of the proper behavior for the "ladies of our family." Suddenly, Ivy glanced up at Robert and me.

"What are you two up to down there? Whispering sweet nothings?" she laughed and took another gulp of wine. "Where's that waiter? Garçon?" Robert shook his head in disgust.

"Well, my aunt's really upset with her," he continued in a low tone.

His aunt was upset, big deal, because my sister, always wanting to be the center of attention, had made an impulsive and thoughtless remark. And it was our wedding rehearsal dinner, the night before our marriage. Shouldn't the bride and groom be the center of attention? The focus was starting to feel all wrong to me: dominating aunt versus bossy sister.

"Crab cakes," I said.

"What?" Robert asked.

"I feel like crab cakes," I answered.

"You hate fish."

"That, and red wine, and this, all of this. Excuse me." I got up and walked toward the ladies' room to re-group.

Standing alone in front of the shell-lined restroom mirror, I thought about it. The whole thing was silly. I'd simply go to the booth, squeeze in beside Aunt Lucy, and apologize for my sister. I'd explain that yes, although she was highly educated, she made the dumbest jokes. I'd face this problem head on, like a woman. It was time I learned to be strong, to speak up, like my new family to be. I opened the door and moved down the dark, long hallway, past the fishnets and Neptune's maidens, towards the booth, my courage draining out with each step. A hand shot out of the darkness, clamped me on the shoulder. I shuddered.

"Come here, want to talk to you for a moment," a low, husky voice commanded. I turned around to see my future father-in-law, Franco. As I followed him down the hallway, I noticed his shoulders were as wide as an apartment-sized refrigerator. He was a formidable, stocky man, who ran a small family business that made lots of money. He was the head of my husband's family, and I had never heard anyone, even my strong-willed fiancé, refuse one of his requests. I followed him as he took me to the bar, motioned me to sit next to him. "Whadda you have?" he asked, several glasses of wine apparent in his speech.

"A glass of rosé?" I squeaked.

"She'll have a whiskey on the rocks. Make it a double, for the both of us," he ordered the bartender. I waited for the lecture on Ivy. Why was I always having to explain her actions to everyone? Wasn't this all wrong? Shouldn't the younger sister be the one screwing up all the time? I hoped he'd understand it was a joke. He leaned in and put his arm around me, looked me in the eye.

"Lacy," his voice was hoarse from years of smoking. "You know what an Italian divorce is?" I breathed a sigh of relief. This would be easy. A pop quiz. I'd dodged the lecture.

"No, sir, I don't."

"Don't call me sir," he commanded. "Call me Dad."

"Sorry, Dad," I answered. He was starting to like me. Maybe he'd rub off on the others, his Sicilian women who were as icy as gelato. "Tell me."

He made his right hand into the shape of a gun, pointed it at my temple.

"An Italian divorce is a bullet in the head," he deadpanned. Was this his idea of a joke? I wasn't sure. I let the curl of a smile begin at the corners of my mouth.

"I mean it," he said. "Don't you ever hurt my boy."

I put on my sincere face. "I wouldn't dream of it, sir—Dad." Apparently for my husband's family, "till death do us part" had a different meaning.

"Good," he replied. "Let's get back to the table before the food comes." Feeling dazed, and understanding for the first time what the word "incredulous" actually meant, I followed.

My booth, my laughing sisters, best friend, and Mama, were all a safe harbor as I slid in. Robert had returned to his family, and my crab cakes were getting cold. In my haste to exit, I hadn't changed my order. I hated crab cakes. I hated this night. I wanted to leave, turn into one of Neptune's mermaids and swim off into the Pacific, away from his crazy family, away from my crazy family, away from Robert. I felt, and tasted, salty tears starting up. I wouldn't allow myself to cry. I wouldn't allow his family to see me shaken. I'd be tough. I felt someone looking at me. I steeled myself and looked over, expecting to see Aunt Lucy finding more fault with me. But as I looked up, I saw Robert's tender eyes filled with concern.

We stepped out onto the balcony away from the others and faced each other to talk it out.

"Are you okay?" he asked. And then all at once it bubbled out of me. I told him about my resentment of his controlling aunt, my embarrassment of my tactless sister, the alienation I felt from him, and how I'd never been so confused.

"I feel the same way, too," he said.

"Like the Hatfields and the McCoys?"

"Without the guns," he replied. Then I remembered Franco's remark about shooting me. I had to tell Robert.

"Robert, your father really frightens me," I said. "He actually threatened to shoot me, should I ever, and I quote, 'hurt his boy.'"

A look of surprise crossed Robert's face; he tossed his head back and laughed. I pulled away.

"Well, I don't think it's funny, not one bit." I could feel my anger down low, starting to well up.

"Don't you see? It's a joke. My dad always tells the bride that, at every wedding he's ever been to."

"It's a sick joke," I replied. "And I didn't like it one bit."

"Yeah, kind of like Ivy's joke about my chubby cousin," he responded.

I looked over at my sister, laughing much too loudly as she slugged back another glass of burgundy, at his father, waving his unlit cigarette in the air as he captivated his family with a story of the old country. And then it hit me. "You're right. My sister, your dad, they both tell lousy jokes. Our families are far from perfect," I held it out as a peace offering.

He nibbled. "Yeah, and they could all learn to take a joke." He reached out to stroke my arm. "Plus, everyone's really tense, especially us."

And that's all it took, his touch. I turned and let his arms enfold me.

As we stood on the balcony, I burrowed into his embrace, away from the damp chill of the night air. I heard muffled laughter from the tables, the blended noise of our two unique and flawed families. The roar of the incoming sea cancelled out the sound of their voices.

California

HIATUS

Wyatt was north of forty and lived south of Sunset on the edge of a canyon where deer sometimes grazed. His 850 square-feet box of a house was squeezed between a McMansion and a McMansion in progress. In fact, the pounding of a hammer is what had woken him up at 6:59 one Tuesday morning.

Wyatt went to the window and lifted the blind to look at the men moving around like ants on his neighbor's partly torn off roof. He cocked his fingers into a trigger and aimed at them. Before he had a chance to make the "bang bang" sound he found so satisfying, the doorbell rang. He quickly threw on his gray jogging pants and answered.

It was his neighbor, Tiffany, the queen of next-door's construction, dressed in work boots and wearing a yellow hard hat.

"Hi ya doin' Wyatt?" she asked. He rubbed his eyes dramatically.

"Am I still dreaming?" he asked.

"I know how you feel, it is early, isn't it? But the sooner we get them going, the sooner we can get our project finished."

"Your project, not mine," he said.

"Yes, but it will improve all our property values, yours too." The discussion was taking a decidedly déjà vu turn. Whatever Tiffany wanted was good for the entire neighborhood, or so she thought.

She glanced past him, peered into his narrow hallway lined with boxes of old head shots, resumes, scripts, and demo reels. He moved his freckled, not-so-chiseled chest in front of her to block her prying eyes.

"So did you stop by to tell me about my rising property value, or what?" Wyatt asked. Force of habit, he fluttered his long eyelashes (once called "emotional and powerful" by a casting director) as he spoke. Tiffany did not seem to notice and continued ahead in her sing-song voice.

"The lumber truck is arriving in half an hour, and we need the spot out front freed up. Could you move your car into your driveway?"

"Actually, Tiff, I haven't even taken a--"

"Ten minutes will work," she said and turned to go.

Wyatt took his good, sweet time, and half an hour later he climbed into his '05 325i. As he turned the key, he looked in his rear view mirror and saw Tiffany sitting in her parked black Explorer waiting to pounce into his space. He muttered to himself as he drove away. "All yours, Tiffy."

At the health club he jogged on a treadmill crammed in between two young women exercising while they read scripts. Probably actresses, possibly producers. He tried to screen them out by looking through the big glass windows with a view of the coastline. Next time he would jog on the beach. He looked up and saw the scrim of brown hugging the Pacific, and nixed that idea. L.A. air—even here on the coast—was filthy, especially in the July heat. Later when he squeezed into the steam room, waited in line for a shower, and ate breakfast wedged into a long row of pretty faces and pungent bodies, he wondered if the health club's filtered air was worth feeling so hemmed in.

Driving east on Sunset, he contemplated living another day with no auditions or callbacks. And what exactly had that last casting director meant by, "We're not looking for triceratops"? He glanced in the rear view mirror. He didn't look that old, but in Hollywood, forty-five was ancient history for an actor who had not yet made it. What Wyatt really wanted to do was to check in with his agent. He would not for fear of again being called a pest. He would simply keep up his normal routine and not let this endless waiting get to him.

So he stopped at the dry cleaners to pick up his blue striped shirt just in case something developed.

Since it was Tuesday, it was time to purchase his four weekly lottery tickets. Four dollars was a cheap price to put a little hope in his pocket. If he won, he would make his own bloody movie and cast himself as the lead. He swung by the market up the street and bought the lottery tickets and a copy of the local newspaper.

Back in his house, he sat in a worn recliner by the front window and, to the accompaniment of sawing and hammering, read the newspaper. He liked reading the "help wanted" ads to see what type of jobs he might be forced to take should this dry spell continue. Would the "professional couple seeking English-speaking nanny" ever consider a man who had once modeled in underwear commercials?

He read an article on mountain lions and learned their numbers were dwindling in the L.A. area. A male had killed the female, leaving their kittens still alive wandering around in the mountain ranges. Wyatt looked out his open front window, past the row of houses and cars, up towards the Santa Monica Mountains that lay in the distance and thought about the wild creatures that lived so close, whose numbers were threatened by their increasingly boxed-in environment. A few weeks earlier, late one arid afternoon, he had spotted a coyote coming down the street. Shabby, thin, and wary, the coyote had stopped and lapped up the sprinkler runoff at the curb out front before heading through Wyatt's back yard and down into the canyon in search of prey. Wyatt had felt nothing but disgust for this ragged-looking creature, partly because during his years in the canyon he'd lost several cats to coyotes. Mountain lions seemed different, somehow noble, as they faced possible extinction. The future of the mountain lion seemed as bleak as his own. He and the mountain lion were brothers in suffering, stuck in L.A. but not really fitting in anymore. Wyatt decided he would spend his hiatus trying to see a mountain lion.

For the next several weeks Wyatt hiked the Temescal Loop Trail where tracks had been spotted. He started up a steep path that led to a view of the ocean. He puffed hard as he climbed up the side of the mountain and frequently stopped to rest and stare into thickets looking for signs of a mountain lion—matted-down grass or paw prints. He saw only smaller creatures, birds or squirrels, sometimes a rabbit, and the occasional lizard or snake.

He quickly tired of the trails populated with joggers and hikers, especially on the weekends. Soon he determined the best time to hike was at dawn or right before dusk. At six feet two inches, Wyatt walked tall and was not afraid of being attacked by a cougar. He had weighed the odds—an attack occurred about every two years in California—against the benefit, solitude. In the faint light between dark and light, the noises of the woods took over: birds hopping in the undergrowth, scampering lizards, and an occasional animal call. He liked being alone and enjoyed the extra oxygen created by the trees and chaparral. And every time he hiked, the trail proved easier with his increasing stamina. Soon he started to lean out.

The long daylight hours of his hiatus continued, punctuated by the chaos of his neighbor's construction. His agent did not call, and he did not win the lottery. Instead, Tiffany appeared at his door with her daily parking requests and other odd business. One day she came over to tell him his gardener had trimmed the trees down too far, and that the cut and bare limbs were not aesthetically pleasing. Another day she appeared bearing rat traps filled with poison and asked Wyatt to put them out in his yard. The squirrels were ruining her garden.

"They're just giant rodents, you know. And they can ruin our gardens. Them and the deer that wander up from the canyon."

"I have no garden," he said. "And I like squirrels chattering," he said. "Drowns out the sound of the hammering." She tilted her head to the side and scrunched up her face.

"Did you lose some weight?" she asked.

She actually looked kind of sexy, but he hated that yellow hard hat.

Soon he set out to escape her constant demands, the construction mess, and the heat by hiding out in the library. It was comforting to be where he did not have to be in a constant state of expectancy for his agent's call. He found a carrel apart from the always crowded tables and sat for hours reading about the habits of mountain lions, also called panthers, cougars, pumas, or catamounts. He looked at pictures of their tracks, larger than the coyote's and with three lobes on the hind edge of the heel pad. Cougars were silent in their journey through the mountain territory and carefully avoided stepping on leaves or twigs so their prey would be unaware. Wyatt couldn't learn enough about the elegant, tawny creatures who were at the top of the food chain in the mountains, if you didn't count man. One night Wyatt skipped an acting workshop to hear a biologist speak on the big cats.

The lecture hall was packed. An odd assortment of people who had their own reasons for wanting to learn more about the stately creatures whose lives blurred into the borders of the growing city. Wyatt stood alone along the back wall and observed.

The biologist gave a slide show and explained that the mountain lions traveled in a fixed territory, or range, spanning over many miles, sometimes up to a hundred square miles. Some of the cougars had been fitted with tracking devices, and it seemed each adult lion traversed a wide loop over and over. Each lion lived a solitary life, in his own territory, coming together only to mate. (Now that made sense—getting along with females out of the bedroom had always been a problem for Wyatt, too.) Encroaching development had begun to cut into the lions' territories and their food supply, primarily deer. The narrowing of their territory could lead to fighting among the lions. A male had recently fought and killed a female either while mating or from fighting over prey.

The summer heat and lack of water had caused all the animals to move closer to neighborhoods in search of sustenance. Sometimes cougars were forced to eat coyotes for lack of other prey. And since coyotes ate smaller creatures that often ingested rat poison, the mountain lion eating a coyote could end up ingesting poison. And if the poison were the anti-coagulant type, the lion could bleed to death.

Following the lecture, Wyatt examined a display of the rat poisons that were indirectly killing mountain lions. One of the boxes looked familiar; it was yellow, the type used by a certain yellow-helmeted neighbor. Wyatt knew what he had to do.

After he returned home, he changed into all black and peeked out his window to see if Tiffany's lights were off. They were, although it was only ten thirty. He speculated that she went to bed early, so she could get up to greet the workmen who always arrived just after dawn. Carrying an old pillowcase, he crouched down as he headed into her yard. He crawled through her aesthetically pleasing garden and ran his hands along the cool soil in search of the rat traps. Next to some ornamental cabbages, he found the first trap and placed it in his pillowcase. He suddenly became aware of someone staring at him. He looked back towards Tiffany's house, but her lights were still off, and there was no activity. He continued his important work of saving the mountain lions, indirectly of course. The work was slow and tedious, running his hands along the soil and moving his fingers in between the stems of her numerous plants. The sharp blades of the sea grass cut his fingers, and he wondered why he hadn't thought to wear gloves.

Over the next hour, he removed nine traps. He finished searching her yard and almost left to go home. Kneeling at the edge of her garden, he stared across the garden towards her grandiose, almost finished second story hulking against the starry night sky. Everything about the woman was overkill, so surely she would have gone beyond the boundaries of her property with her rat trap project. He started down the canyon slopes, moving his hands along the gravelly ground below the undergrowth. Sure enough he found another trap. The woman's spilling into the canyon infuriated Wyatt. How far did her arrogance extend?

Fueled by the thoughts of Tiffany and her mega-mansion and her mega-poison, her total lack of boundaries, Wyatt grew more intent in his mission, crawling further from her property line. A full thirty feet below her yard he found yet another rat trap! What was she trying to do? Poison every animal in the wilderness? He thought about the mountain lions, or possibly the kittens, he was saving by providing an untainted food supply. He was overcome with a fierceness on behalf of his threatened brothers in suffering, hemmed in by the encroaching mass of people and houses that is L.A.

Wyatt was startled when he felt the sharp pain in the back of his neck, surprised as he felt his body being dragged down into the canyon. He tried to fight, but the thing that had grabbed him from behind was much larger. Before his spinal cord was severed, he forgave the noble mountain lion for simply acting on instinct.

Wyatt would have been happy to know his agent managed to show up at his memorial service a week later, along with the mountain lion crowd, a few assorted friends, acquaintances really, and two TV news crews. Tiffany insisted on giving a eulogy where she told of their mutual efforts to remove the rat poison. Had she not had a bad cold that night, she would have been with him, she said. The mountain lion crowd didn't seem to believe her, but Wyatt's agent gave her a card and asked her if she had done any acting. And that night when the story came on the news, a director who lived in the next canyon over saw Wyatt's picture on TV and remarked to his wife that Wyatt's demise was a shame.

"You know, he could have played the aging bodyguard on that new series we're shooting in September."

"He looks too young to me," she said.

"Maybe," said the director. "And did you see those eyelashes?"

California

BACKYARD MESSAGES

At first the woman sweeping the porch did not see anything in the tree high above the back yard, but when she stopped her sweeping to look up at the morning sun spilling through the tree top she saw a thick, upright form that was not part of the dark, gray-brown branches. She ran inside to the laundry room to retrieve her glasses from her purse, came back out and studied the thing sitting on the black elm tree limb. It was about a foot and a half tall and had gray tufts of feathers on either side of its head that looked like ears, or horns.

"El tecolote," Lucero whispered and clutched her hand over the crucifix that hung over her generous bosom. She could not believe her good fortune, but she did not have time to dwell on it. There were clothes to wash, floors to sweep, beds to make. After she had finished sweeping the porch, she looked up again to see el tecolote staring at her with its yellow-orange eyes. She went inside the ranch house to do her work but ran outside often to see if he was still there. Every time she looked up, he would swivel his head around and stare at her with those startlingly bold and wide eyes. By noon, when her employer finally came out to the patio and joined Lucero for lunch, he was gone.

The two women sat down at the wrought iron table on the cleanly swept patio to eat the Salvadoran rice Lucero had cooked. Except for their broad, mid-life waistlines, the two women did not look alike. Fair and freckled, Ellen shielded herself from the sun with a wide-brimmed hat; Lucero welcomed the heat of the noon sun against her glowing face and kept her dark, thick hair tied back with a turquoise clasp. They dug into the hot, fragrant rice—a mixture of oil, water, long-grain rice, and chopped vegetables crisped brown in some places, "brown-down," Lucero called it—and did not talk at first as they sated their hunger. At the table on this early September day, they were simply two friends sharing a meal and taking in the view of the lush yard ringed with camellias and bordered on both sides by high trees that gave the yard a sense of privacy.

A crow cawed and flew over. They both looked at the dark intruder, and Lucero spoke.

"I saw el tecolote there this morning," she said. "Owl."

"Where?" asked Ellen. Lucero pointed to the neighbors' tree whose branches extended into Ellen's yard.

"There. On branch over this yard. You yard."

"In the daytime, you saw an owl?" asked Ellen. She thought owls were night birds. Lucero nodded.

"Is good luck," she said. "For person who see it. Not everybody see it."

"Oh, then it's luck for you and not me?" Ellen teased. Lucero smiled and then quickly clarified.

"I see tecolote, but he look at you house. Maybe you have luck and me too," she said diplomatically. They both laughed.

"I could use some luck," said Ellen. She mentally catalogued her recent string of bad luck. Sales had dropped off and money was tight. One of her Manchester terriers had been diagnosed with congestive heart failure. His pills and the vet bills were phenomenal. Although Lucero only came one day a week, she had thought of letting her go but did not want to. Lucero needed the income as much as Ellen needed the companionship. Ellen's misfortune had all seemed to start the previous fall when she had returned from a business trip and found a sick, stray Siamese cat in her back yard. A bad sign, Lucero had told her, and when Ellen wound up paying $150 to have the cat treated, only to have it run away a day later, she agreed. The cat's appearance seemed to have triggered a year of bad luck. Perhaps the sighting of the tecolote would counter it…

Lucero thought of her past year. The granddaughter she'd cared for the past three years had been

reclaimed by her birth mother, just released from pris-
on. So now her home was empty of her angelic eight-
year-old granddaughter, Anna. Yet at home she still
had her own daughter, twenty, who had found a good-
paying job where her bi-lingual skills were appreciat-
ed. And Lucero was grateful to have steady work from
a roster of clients, who, like Ellen, seemed too busy
or did not want to clean their own houses. Good luck
could bring her money enough to move from her one-
bedroom apartment near the freeway where she lived
with her daughter and another mother and daughter.
Perhaps her coming good fortune brought by el tecolote would enable her to buy a house with a garden
where something always bloomed, a yard like this one
that Ellen did not seem to have much time to enjoy...

That night when Ellen went to let the dogs out
into her back yard, she thought of the owl that Lucero
had seen. Would the creature dive bomb into her
yard and eat one of her tiny dogs? She listened for the
owl's hooting, but all she heard was the gurgling of
her neighbor's feng shui fountain above the muted
sound of the surf echoing up the canyon. Later, after
she had collected the dogs and tucked them into their
dog beds, she went to her bedroom on the other side
of the house. She lay in her bed by the open window
under the big sycamore and tried to fall asleep while
she thought of the owl, and luck, and fortune, and misfortune, and superstition. She remembered lying by
this same window—was it last night? She had heard

a hooting noise from across the opposite canyon, or so she had assumed. Sound traveled in the canyons—barking dogs, yelping coyotes, music from the bands playing at the nearby country club, and occasionally a random gunshot in the night. When she heard the hooting owl, probably the same one Lucero had spied in the black elm tree, the sound had emanated not from the canyon but from right in her own back yard. Lucero had noticed, but she had not. Perhaps we are the last to see our own potential good fortune, Ellen thought as she drifted off.

Lucero did not ponder her possible good luck but rather acted upon it, stopping on the way home to buy nine lotto scratchers at the liquor store when she transferred buses. She tucked the tickets in her purse and waited till after she had cooked supper to see if the luck the owl had brought her had come to pass. Later, lying in her bed listening to her daughter's soft snoring and the roar of the passing cars on the freeway, she thought about the money she had won with the scratchers and reassured herself that with luck, one had to be patient.

The following week, Lucero and Ellen were on the back patio again enjoying Salvadorian rice and looking up at the bare branches of the black elm. No owl was there.

"Tell me more about the owl," Ellen said.

"The one I see, was tecolote. In Salvador, my grandmamma tell me it lucky." Lucero explained there was also a bad owl, lechuza, which was gray or white and smaller. Seeing lechuza would bring death to the one who saw it. Lucero reassured Ellen the owl that had made its recent appearance was the good one.

"When I tell the people in Spanish, they say, 'Oh my God, you saw where?' I tell them here."

"Did you have any luck?" Ellen asked. Lucero nodded.

"Yes, I won six dollars at scratchers."

"Good," Ellen said. "I'm glad you got the luck."

"Me too."

"How many tickets did you buy?" Ellen asked.

"Nine," Lucero answered, and smiled. Ellen looked puzzled for a moment.

"So you spent nine dollars and won six?" Ellen asked.

"Yes," Lucero nodded. And they both laughed.

California

UNDER MILKWEED LEAVES

A week before I was to move away from Los Angeles, I thought to drive north one last time to Goleta and the butterfly groves. It was November, near the time when thousands of monarch butterflies were expected to arrive for their annual stay in a small forest of eucalyptus not far from the Pacific Ocean.

I was in no rush to get there—it was mid-afternoon, and my son, Trevor, promised he and his new friend would meet me there after work, just before sunset. I would meander up the coast route past Point Magu, then cut inward through the fields of crops and the smells I loved—dirt and sometimes strawberries or onions.

It was a familiar route—the 1 leading to the 101—I had driven so regularly in the six years since my son had left home for college in Santa Barbara.

In that time, so much had happened along the way, and yet so much had stayed the same. At twenty-four, Trevor was still in Santa Barbara, done with college, working full-time, and living with a houseful of roommates. Mudslides had narrowed the lanes of the coast highway for a time, and fragile-looking nets had been placed along the hillsides in an attempt to hold back rocks and earth. In Camarillo, farm workers wearing bright hats and scarves tended the crops that had nourished me for the two decades that I had lived in southern California. I always mouthed a word of thanks as I drove past them, a dozen or so men and women bent over green rows of vegetables. At Oxnard, I passed my old friend, the plastic Santa Claus statue that stood between a used car lot and a trailer park. After a bad case of termites, his handlers had moved him away from Santa Claus Lane in Carpinteria. Now, there was no Santa statue on Santa Claus Lane.

I headed up the 101, past the beaches of Ventura and hang gliders dangling near the coastal mountain range, onward to where the road hugs the coast, to where the blue-green of the Pacific is punctuated with oil platforms on the horizon. Above the freeway I saw the sign for San Francisco that always tempts me to keep on driving. I never do.

The air grew sweeter, my spirit lightened, the further I got away from Los Angeles and the closer I

came to the place where butterflies land to over winter. I pulled off the highway and found my way to the
residential neighborhood of Ellwood that lies near the
entrance to the groves. A dusty path through scrubby
terrain took me to some placards telling the monarchs' story.

Much is known about these fragile gold and orange
creatures, yet some things remain a mystery. They fly
over from somewhere west of the Rocky Mountains, or
perhaps points north, returning every October to the
Australian eucalyptus groves in Goleta. After resting
there for a few months, they unite in mid-air to mate,
then fall to the ground coupled together. The males
die soon after; the females flutter away to lay their eggs
before dying. This generation of butterflies will not
make it back home. Their offspring's offspring will continue on the migration path, somehow knowing which
direction to go. Even the scientists have not figured out
exactly how the butterflies know which way to go.

I continued walking past a creaking and groaning
stand of eucalyptus, headed for Ellwood Main, a large
grove of trees ringed by a low rope to keep away human intruders. No one was in sight, and the grove was
as quiet as an empty cathedral.

"Please do not disturb the monarchs as they mate,"
a sign instructed. Why was it so easy for butterflies to
find a mate but so difficult for people? Why couldn't
Trevor find a girl who really cared for him?

I hated moving so far away, all the way to London, leaving my son alone except for his roommates and no one special. He was very guarded about his romantic life. I remembered the time a year earlier when Trevor had snapped at me after I had tried to introduce him to a friend's daughter. She was, he said, not his type at all. He could find his own dates. I had tried to stop wondering what his type might be. Probably smart, perhaps a brunette, definitely a non-smoker. When I called to tell him I was driving up to Goleta to see the monarchs, he said he had someone he wanted me to meet. I secretly hoped this one might be the one.

Wandering along the forest's perimeter, I stayed outside the roped-off area and scanned the green limbs and gray bark for butterflies. With their wings folded in, and hanging from the slender eucalyptus trees, the monarchs can sometimes be hard to see. As I moved closer, I spotted them, colorful clusters dangling from the limbs, nature's ornaments. In the hush of the woods, thousands of them hung together, warmed by their collective body heat.

In the grove, there's an opening in the tree tops called a "magic circle" where the sun comes through. As the temperature shifts throughout the day, butterflies fly in and out of this "magic circle" warming themselves in shafts of sunlight as needed. I stared up at the break in the canopy, at this circle of blue sky and light ringed by the stately eucalyptus trees. I was rewarded with the sight of a single butterfly drifting toward the tall branches, returning to this place that was now his home.

With no sign of my son, I decided to take a quick hike out to the ocean view bluffs to see the sunset. I headed along the path leading out of the butterfly groves toward a grassy meadow that smelled of sea and tar. A seagull flew overhead, and a seal barked in the distance. I heard muffled voices ahead of me and looked up. In the smoky half-light of the forest I made out the silhouette of a couple walking towards the grove, their arms linked together. In the waning light, the two of them looked like a giant butterfly descending into the forest. And then I heard a man's voice—Trevor's—and another voice—also a man's. They laughed together. A happy couple, a couple who looked like they cared for one another, but not the one I had imagined. I felt a shifting inside, old expectations making way for new realizations. My emotions threatened to tumble out of control. I struggled to hold them back. I felt as ineffective as one of those delicate nets I had seen along the hillsides on the coast highway.

The couple moved closer. The taller one waved.

"Hi, Mom," Trevor called. "I got off early and we took a hike to the bluffs." He pulled away from the other man and walked over to give me a hug. His big hands felt warm on my shoulders, and he gave me an extra squeeze. He was, and always would be, my son.

"Is this your," I hesitated, trying to find the right word. "Friend?"

"I thought you knew," Trevor said, and introduced me to a willowy young man wearing double earrings in his left ear.

"This is Edward," he said. I felt so awkward and unsure. I extended my hand to Edward, took hold of his slender hand, and shook hands. I had never felt a gentler handshake, so different from Trevor's sturdy grip.

"Good to meet you," he said. He looked me in the eye as he spoke.

"I'm pleased to meet you, too," I said, meaning it and at last understanding so much. Trevor's reaction when I had tried to set him up, his secretiveness about his social life, his decision to stay on in Santa Barbara after graduation. Trevor coughed and Edward let go of my hand to reach for something in his backpack. He pulled out a water bottle. They exchanged a smile as Trevor took it from him.

"The pollens bother him when we hike," Edward said.

"And he always gives me water," Trevor said before upending the bottle and taking a gulp. Edward watched him drink and as I saw, I felt myself softening towards this man who so clearly cared for my son.

"Have you seen the monarchs?" Edward asked.

"Yes," I said. "Aren't they magnificent?" Edward nodded and then continued.

"They love it up here in the eucalyptus groves because the Asclepias—milkweed—is nearby. The

females lay their eggs under milkweed leaves so preda-
tors won't get them."

"Acting on instinct," I said.

"Exactly," Edward answered.

"He's a bio major," said Trevor, "in case you hadn't
noticed." He offered me one hand and took Edward's
in his other. The three of us walked back towards the
grove, Trevor in the middle.

"Look at that," Trevor said, pointing up at the sky
where the light filtered down. We stopped and turned
our gaze upward, to the magic circle.

Two monarchs floated above, their translucent
orange-yellow wings kissed by sunlight. Steered in
the right direction by nature's compass, the pair flew
toward the welcoming branches of the eucalyptus.
There, they would be safe and warm together in their
winter home.

EUROPE

Belgium

POSTCARDS FROM BRUGES

That afternoon, although I did not want to go, we were leaving Bruges, a city of thousand-year-old cathedrals, churches, bridges, and canals. On the canal tour, and later the horse carriage trip around the city, I had allowed the ancient buildings and bridges to distract me from dark thoughts. The city was a place out of time that gave me an almost smug feeling. While death could take me, it had not altered these stone buildings.

My son, Jeff, and I stood side-by-side staring at an ancient carved stone face that adorned one of the medieval buildings along a cobblestone street. The gargoyle mouthed a silent scream. Mute in its anguish, I thought but did not say.

"It reminds me of Edvard Munch's *The Scream*," I said. "No wonder people back then believed gargoyles would keep away evil spirits."

"Grotesques," he said.

"I'd say ugly, but not grotesque."

"No, Mother, they're called grotesques. Gargoyles are a type of fountain. Everything else is a grotesque."

"Is there anything you don't know?" I asked. Jeff was a master of factoids. He knew everything about anything, except he did not know what I had learned just before our departure for Belgium and the Netherlands. I had not found the courage to tell him. And since we had arrived in Belgium, Jeff, a self-focused 24, had not seemed to notice I was less interested than usual in his lengthy, detailed descriptions of architecture and history. Instead, I found myself distracted by the morbid, such as the gargoyles, or the graves that lay under the floor inside the Béguinage church. While Jeff adjusted his light meter to photograph some statuary, I stood atop the rich people's tombstones that made up the floor, pondering where I would be buried. Or would I be cremated?

I was uncertain how my passing would affect Jeff. Caught up in his turbulent twenties, he was trying to find his way in the world, muddling through college, toying with alcohol and lifestyles, trying to figure out who, and what, he wanted. Although I realized I could not choose his path, I was concerned about my still-evolving son, worried I would not be there for him if he needed me. Worst of all, I had not figured out how to tell him what the doctors had told me: my cancer had returned.

Since we arrived on the continent, I had been waiting for the right moment to tell him. I had imagined
that the beauty of our surroundings would somehow
soften my ugly news, that the cancer was back, and I
was unwilling to once again engage in chemotherapy's
ugly dance, although the doctors had suggested it as a
last resort.

The opportune time to tell him, if there were such
a thing, had eluded me. In Brussels, I had thought
to explain it over beer (his fourth, my second) in the
Mort Subite Café where he'd carefully translated the
words for me.

"Sudden death," he declared, hoisting his beer to
his lips. Instead of telling him then, I'd chosen to jest
that I hoped the "sudden death" didn't refer to what
would happen to him if he drank too much, not an
invalid concern considering all he had imbibed on this
trip.

Inebriated, or not, there had been no right moment to share my grim news. Or maybe there had.
Maybe I had chosen not to tell him because I could
not stand the thought of seeing his face contort with
pain. I remembered the pain etched on his face when
his father had left us; Jeff was six, and I, twenty-eight,
much too young, I felt, to go it alone as a single parent.
Yet in the years that followed, my son and I had grown
closer and leaned on each other through much of his
growing up, and mine. Once Jeff left for college, I was
careful to give him space, not to burden him with my

troubles. Now this incomprehensible, toxic garbage truck of a burden I bore alone was much too big to unload on him, even though I knew I must in order to prepare him.

"Come on, Mother. We need to hustle if we want to make the 11:00 a.m. train," he said, pulling me into the present. Towing my small suitcase behind me, I followed my son over the rough cobblestones towards the bus stop that would take us to the Bruges train station, and on to Amsterdam.

There, we would visit the Van Gogh Museum and see the originals of the scenes I had long loved. Jeff would drop in the coffee shops and smoke grass and possibly buy other drugs. What he did not know was that I planned to accompany him. Why not? I thought. The wildly replicating cancer cells had freed me of all notions of propriety and what was right or wrong. Like Amsterdam, I had adopted my own social tolerance policy. When you are dying, anything goes.

We arrived at the train station and headed up to the platform to await the train to Antwerp. We passed the time on a bench writing out postcards, Jeff to several of his friends and I to mine. I felt someone staring at us, and looked up to see an older, portly man wearing a dark hat and suit with a black overcoat. He carried a briefcase. A businessman on a journey, with some greenery wrapped in cellophane, tucked under his arm.

The train arrived. Jeff and I stepped aboard and made our way down the aisle. He was stowing our bags above when I looked up to see the man in the black coat standing in the aisle next to our seats.

"Are you American?" he asked. Jeff and I hesitated before answering. Since we'd arrived in Belgium, because of anti-American sentiment and terrorism in the Netherlands, we found it best to let people assume we were German, or French. I saw Jeff size up the man's direct stare, his serious expression, before answering.

"Yes, we're American," Jeff said.

"Me too," he said. He turned to take off his hat, revealing a partial head of white hair. I took a seat by the window and pulled down the tray table, so I could finish writing my postcards. Jeff sat down next to me, across from the man in the black suit.

"Where are you from in the States?" he asked.

"California," Jeff answered.

"I'm from Marina Del Rey," he said.

"What a coincidence," Jeff said.

"A coincidence is when God has done something, but he doesn't want you to know," he said. Jeff and I nodded, yet I saw Jeff shifting uneasily in his seat. It was too early in the morning for a spiritual conversation, especially for my skeptical son.

In the next ten minutes, we found out the man's name, Thomas Taylor, and his opinion on the upcoming elections. When Jeff asked what he was doing in

Belgium, he pointed to a train-shaped postcard I was working on and explained he was a postcard salesman.

"My company made that one," he said. His postcards were not ordinary, he said. They came in all sizes and shapes such as houses, mountaintops, boats, and trains. His cards cost more because people would pay for quality. He had spent the last thirty years traveling all over Europe distributing his product. A traveling postcard salesman, we found out later, on the way to synagogue in Antwerp to celebrate Sukkot.

"There is no synagogue in Bruges," he said, holding up the palm, willow, and a lemon-like branch. He explained the Sukkot tradition of bringing a gift to God. He had been celebrating for days and announced, while patting his rounded belly, that he had put on a few kilos over the holiday. We rolled through the lush Belgian countryside filled with abundant trees. The train rocked over the rails, and I listened to this stranger telling Jeff of his life, and philosophy, while I wrote out each postcard, carefully affixing a stamp before moving to the next. The postcard salesman saw, and leaned over to speak to me.

"Those stamps won't work after you leave Belgium," he said.

"I guess you'd know," said Jeff. "You're the expert." Mr. Taylor nodded.

"We'll be sure to mail them in Antwerp," Jeff said.

"Sometimes our best intentions go astray," Mr. Taylor said.

"We should have enough time between trains," Jeff said. "Is there a mailbox on the platform?"

"I'm not sure," Mr. Taylor said. "Can I mail them for you when I get off at Antwerp?"

"Are you sure it's not too much trouble?" asked Jeff.

"Not at all," Mr. Taylor responded. "What good is a message if not delivered?"

"I'm not done yet," I said, reluctant to hand over my cards to an almost stranger. I wrote out another.

For the next hour or so, Mr. Taylor regaled us with his life history while I looked at him and the changing scenery in the window that framed his face. Farmhouses with step-gabled roofs, cows, huge draft horses, rows of purple and bright green cabbages. Everything laid out in an orderly, and perfect, fashion, like Mr. Taylor's life story, it seemed. I was content to watch and listen, glad to see Jeff engaged in a lively discussion with someone other than me for a change.

"I wasn't always Jewish, you know. I came to it late in life."

"What were you before?" Jeff asked.

"Nothing," he answered.

"An agnostic?" Jeff asked. Mr. Taylor nodded. He went on to explain how he served in the Marines, and later, sold name tags.

"You know those plastic name badges? I brought them to Vegas and from there, to all the conventions, all over the world." In Tel Aviv on a business trip in the '70s, and on the advice of a friend, Mr. Taylor had gone to see a rabbi. Together, Mr. Taylor and the rabbi opened the Torah to find a random verse.

"He told me I'd see a sign in the reading," said Mr. Taylor. "It was the story of Joshua and Caleb, their return from Canaan with a big bunch of grapes. You know the story?" I saw Jeff nod although I was sure he did not know the story. He was an avid reader, but he had not read the Bible and had in fact once called it a huge fairy tale. The postcard salesman explained how Joshua and Caleb were sent out to spy on Canaan, along with some others. They returned with a branch so heavy with grapes it had to be carried on a staff between them. The other spies who made the journey did not believe they could conquer the lands and fight against the giants who lived there. They were punished for their lack of faith and never allowed to enter the Promised Land. Only Caleb and Joshua had faith and courage God would see them through as he promised. They believed, traveled to the land of milk and honey, and were rewarded with long lives. Caleb lived to 85 and Joshua to 110.

It was easy to imagine this story with the passing backdrop behind Mr. Taylor as he spoke. A herd of sheep moved slowly, determinedly across a field. Behind them, dense rain clouds clustered, and the sky darkened. I pointed at the thunderheads.

"Rain is predicted," said Mr. Taylor, and continued his story.

"My brother died on Rosh Hashanah, the judgment day. He didn't believe. This got me to thinking. Soon after, my mother died, and after that, my marriage failed. It all seemed hopeless. Then I remembered the story of Joshua and Caleb. I re-read it and believed I could overcome with God's help. I converted to Judaism. And my faith has shown me, despite all my past failures and troubles, that there is good in life." Jeff nodded politely, but I had to speak up.

"How do you explain all the bad in the world?" I asked.

"Such as?" he asked.

"War, terrorism, suffering. Dying."

"Your pain depends on the context it's in. For example, in Antwerp there have been many anti-Semitic incidents, violent attacks."

"Targeting orthodox Jews," Jeff added.

"Right," said Taylor.

"So how can you believe there is good in the world, knowing one of your friends might be blown up on the way to temple?" I asked. Even Jeff seemed appalled at my question, but Mr. Taylor simply nodded and continued.

"Like I was saying, it's all in the context. If someone were shot on the way to temple, their pain in the moment would be hard to bear, but in the big scheme of things, in the context of eternal life, their pain happens for a very short time. Soon the suffering will be over. The pain will be gone, and they'll have the rest of eternity. Pain is transient." I disagreed, but didn't say so.

"That's an interesting perspective," Jeff said.

"It's my job to be a Jew, to share my beliefs with others," Mr. Taylor answered.

Jeff looked perplexed. "Isn't that a Christian notion?"

"It's my mission," he said, leaning in and lowering his voice.

"You know, I once was hypnotized, and it turns out I was a Jewish slave under Titus the Second. I bought my freedom and joined the Romans."

"Hmmm," said Jeff. "That's really interesting."

Behind Taylor, the scenery disappeared, replaced by the dark walls of a tunnel. We were nearing a city. A voice came over the intercom and interrupted our train mate's metaphysical wanderings.

"Antwerpen, Zuid."

"Is that us, Jeff?" I asked.

"Two stops after," he answered.

"Let's gather our things, then," I said. I pulled the postcards out of my pocket.

"We may have to make a run for it to catch a train on another platform," said Jeff. "It could be tight."

"Why don't you let me mail those postcards for you?" Mr. Taylor offered again. Jeff and I looked at each other for a moment. If I didn't give them to the postcard salesman, he could be insulted. But if I did, would he really mail them? If he did not, what would be lost, really? A few stamps and some hurried words? I decided not to turn down the stranger's offer.

"Sure," I said. "Thanks." I handed him the post-cards. He put them in his coat pocket, then stood up, retrieved his bag and cellophane-wrapped Sukkot greenery.

"Antwerpen, Berchem," the announcer said over the train intercom. Mr. Taylor, Jeff and I headed down the aisle, under the watchful eyes of some dreadlocked teenagers headed to the city. Jeff thanked Mr. Taylor for the conversation. I could see he was antsy to move on, away from the discussion of religion, which made him uneasy. We all moved to the front of the car, then to the rocking platform between cars, saying our goodbyes.

"Antwerpen, Centraal" the announcer spoke as we pulled into the station. Suddenly, Mr. Taylor leaned forward, put his arms around Jeff, and hugged him. I watched this unexpected display of affection, heard him say something to Jeff in a low voice. He pulled away from Jeff and then turned to me.

"He is a good boy. He has a pure heart and soul. He'll have a good life." He headed down the stairs, disappeared into the crowd on the platform. Jeff and I went the other way, rushing for the Amsterdam train. We made it with two minutes to spare.

Once we were seated, and I caught my breath, I spoke. "What was all that about?"

"I'm not sure, Mother, but check to make sure your wallet's there."

I laughed, but checked. My wallet was untouched. "Now that we've determined he wasn't a pickpocket, what was he?" I asked.

"An unusual man for sure," Jeff said.

"What did he say when he hugged you?"

"He mumbled, but what I think he said was, 'Forgive me. I once had a son like you.'" We puzzled over Mr. Taylor all the way to Amsterdam. Jeff was certain he was just a postcard salesman, off lithium. I was inclined to agree, except much of what he said had made sense, particularly the part about pain and suffering in my present context. What I most wanted to believe was Mr. Taylor's prediction about Jeff. "He will have a good life."

In Amsterdam, we checked into a small, modern, cramped hotel next to the train station and then headed out to walk along the canals to find a coffee shop. At the Bulldog Café, we ordered cappuccinos, and Jeff bought several joints. After he lit up and smoked for a minute or two, I surprised him by asking if I could take a few puffs. He hesitated at first, but seemed delighted when I blew smoke rings and joked with the bartender. We were relaxed and open, and it was the perfect time to tell him. I could not.

We moved back out on the street amidst the youthful crowds in search of sex and drugs, past the scantily clad prostitutes posing in the picture windows and the frites and ice cream shop with the sign bearing the absurd Manneken Pis brass boy peeing for all to see.

"Hmmm...fries and urine," said Jeff. "What were they thinking?"

"It does seem out of context," I said. "Unless you look at the larger scheme of things." It was almost the right time to tell him, until we looked up at the sign with the golden boy peeing with his not-so-large anatomy. Laughter overcame us.

It was not until much later, back in the states the day after our return, that I finally told him. We were recovering from jet lag, watching CNN when a story came on about an orthodox Jew who had been shot in Antwerp. Jeff wondered if our Mr. Taylor knew the victim. We spoke of him.

"Remember what he said about pain and suffering?" I asked. "He could have been talking about me, Jeff. The cancer's back."

Jeff turned away from the TV, stared at me. For a moment he was silent. His face was contorted with surprise and fear. I thought of the gargoyle I had seen in Bruges.

"I'll go with you to the chemo, Mom. We'll beat it again," he said. I took his hand, told him it was too late. He reached out, enfolded me in his long arms, as Mr. Taylor had done to him before leaving. I remembered what the postcard salesman said about my son:

he's a good boy, he's got a good soul. It was a comfort, especially for someone who was soon to die.

Jeff would not have it. He told me we would fight the cancer together. I told him I could not suffer through the nausea of chemotherapy. He argued that the pain would be transient, that I would survive.

"You sound like a postcard salesman," I said. He shrugged.

"Just try. For me," he said. So it was for him that I found myself with a needle in my vein two weeks later. Jeff was at my side as the toxic chemicals poured into me.

Over the next few months, we faced the battle for my life together. During the hours in the chemotherapy sessions while I lay still and chilled, suffering, when I was at my lowest, Jeff would smile and simply say, "big context," to cheer me on. We spoke often of Mr. Taylor, and made a list of the six postcards he was supposed to mail for us. We questioned if he had really posted them. When Jeff took time to call each of our friends to see if they had gotten their card from Antwerp, all had arrived in good order. The postcard salesman had been true to his word.

Jeff took a leave of absence from college that semester to care for me, and his bar-hopping, wild crowd finally stopped bothering to ask him out. When he wasn't running errands or taking care of me, he started jogging in the park near our home. He drank only an occasional glass of wine with meals and started planning his coursework for the coming semester. He remained close to his friends Sam and Rose, a quiet young couple whom he had met in art history class. They stopped by from time-to-time to bring us a funny DVD and some of Rose's homemade olive bread.

One Saturday afternoon my nausea and weakness brought us to a new low. A final chemotherapy session loomed ahead. I had not been able to hold down more than water for several days, and I had just told Jeff I did not know if I had the courage to continue. There was a knock at the door. It was Rose and Sam, carrying a parcel wrapped in brown paper. Handing it to Jeff, Sam explained.

"It actually came in a larger package, and when I unwrapped it, there was a note that said, 'Sam, please give this to your friend, Jeff.'" Jeff tore open the paper.

"Who's it from?" he asked. Sam shrugged.

"There was no return address, but it had foreign stamps," he said. "How'd the sender know you were my friend, anyway?" Jeff asked. He finished removing the brown paper, revealing a white box, about the size of large shoebox. He paused before lifting the lid.

"Everyone take cover," he said. We all laughed, although Rose actually stepped back a few steps and stood by the door.

"Go ahead, open it," said Sam. Jeff lifted the lid, pulled back some white tissue paper. He lifted out a wooden carving of two men carrying a huge branch of grapes between them.

"What is it?" asked Sam. Jeff ran his hands along the bunch of grapes, set the wooden sculpture on top of the dresser where I could see it from my bed.

"A gift from this nut case we happened to meet on the train," said Jeff.

"Or an angel," I said.

"Peddling postcards," Jeff said.

"And hope," I added. My son, the master of factoids, did not disagree.

Sicily

SAN VITO LO CAPO
(BILLY'S HONEYMOON)

Beads of sweat trace down her butternut arms, travel towards the sultry sand where we lie beside each other on towels. It is so hot here, I next expect to see steam rise off the shiny wet surface of my Francesca's skin. The dry sirocco blowing in from the Sahara Desert reminds me that here on the coast of Sicily we are a mere one hundred fifty kilometers across the water from North Africa. She suddenly turns over, props up on one elbow and stares at me with hazel eyes that reflect the sea. I lean in and kiss her full and warm lips, but only briefly. She pulls away and starts talking.

"Is that him?" she asks. She points towards the Tyrrhenian Sea where a street urchin of twelve, or so, bobs around in the pale aquamarine water. Like my Francesca, he has black hair and beautiful dark skin, but his is marred by a pale scar that runs along his cheek under his eye.

"It's Scarface," I say. She jumps up from the white sand. It sticks to her damp legs like raw sugar. Navigating toward the water, she moves through the throngs of Sicilian couples and families, beckoning me to follow.

"Let's go out where he is," she says. I hesitate. She is wearing the $2 paper-thin dress we purchased the night before from the Moroccan street vendor after realizing our bags had been lost by the airlines. I am wearing an even cheaper pair of street vendor red trunks.

"What about that dress? It will cling to you like saran wrap," I say, while allowing her to pull me into the tepid sea.

"Come on, Billy, he's swimming away," she says. We wade in, and I watch as the thin nylon skirt rises to the surface, floats around her like a lavender lily pad. She giggles and paddles out several yards away from me, towards where the boy plays in the tiny waves breaking along the turquoise surface. I follow her wake as we slice through a school of tiny silver fish. Suddenly she yelps.

"Ow! Was that you?" she shivers and looks down through the clear water.

"Me or a fish. You figure it out," I tease. She splashes me again. I fling my head back, flash her a white-toothy grin she has dubbed my "Prince William Smile."

She laughs at me, and then we hear another laugh. We turn around to see Scarface bobbing in the surf a few yards away. He grins back and yells at us, then dives into a wave and darts away as fast as one of those silver fish.

"What was he saying?" she asks.

"That you have breasts like Aphrodite." Her breasts are full and round and float like globes under the thin wet nylon.

"Billy—please. Be serious," she begs. Francesca's curiosity is the all-consuming kind. When she gets interested in something, she's unstoppable. An occupational hazard. When not honeymooning with me, my wife writes for a fledgling online magazine. She continues.

"I got the first word. It sounded like 'hair ah.' Maybe he was talking about you—your blonde hair."

"Maybe," I answer.

"Or maybe it was 'era'—you know, like we are from a different era. Now that would make sense, since we're, well you are, anyway, quite a bit older than he." I shrug, although at thirty-five, I am only five years older than she.

"I'm kidding. Or maybe he was speaking Italian," she says. "I wish we knew." She treads water and stares at me. What she doesn't speak of is the missing dictionary, now lost somewhere between Los Angeles and Sicily, thanks to British Airways or Alitalia or both.

"Let's get out, go back up to the hotel, and see if the bags have arrived," I suggest.

"You just want to get me back in bed," she says, and ducks under water, out of sight. She's right. I dive below, wrap my arms around her middle and carry her back to shallow water. I throw her over my shoulder, and she pretends to fight.

"Man want woman," I grunt like a Neanderthal and carry her towards our towels. Like a caught fish, she tries to wiggle back into the sea.

"Woman want to hide under towel," she says. I let go of her, and she sinks down into the warm water while I retrieve her towel. I return to the water, and she stands up in the clingy dress. Seeing her, I want to return to our room. At once. I wrap the towel around her and lean in to nibble her ear. She is a willing snack. We head for the hotel and she seems to forget, at least for the moment, about her little scar-faced mystery man.

Passing through the breezy lobby, the uniformed, self-important, and always helpful receptionist, Giorgia, waves us over to her desk. Giorgia speaks slowly and solemnly, trying to find the right words.

"Your bags was in Arizona."

"Arizona?" Francesca and I speak at the same time.

"Yes," she says.

"Well, do you know when they'll arrive?" I ask.

"This night, after dinner. I will inform when they come," Giorgia replies. We walk away, debating whether

or not our bags were really lost in the southwest, or if
Giorgia's English isn't as good as she thinks.

Up in our room, we peel off our cheap, wet street
vendor clothes and jump into a warm shower. Using a
small bar of soap, we lather each other all over. After
we are done, she asks me to put our wet clothes out to
dry, so I wrap a towel around my waist and head out to
the balcony to lay my too small trunks and her flimsy
dress across the deck chairs in the hot sun. I shut the
sliding glass door against the heat and return to the
cool sheets where I entangle my pale limbs with her
dark ones for the next several hours.

Much later, the blue hour approaches as we lie in
bed. Francesca sleeps while I watch her breathe in and
out. I stare through the large window at a bruised blue
sky over teal sea.

Spending our honeymoon here in San Vito lo
Capo was my idea. I thought it would be fun to see the
country where Francesca's great grandparents were
born. To be entirely truthful, what I really wanted was
to be far away from her family and mine, in a place
where we would share the adventure of being the only
Americans in town. Neither of us speaks Italian, but
I had assumed that if we had trouble communicating
with the locals, she and I would simply cuddle together
over our dictionary, sounding out unfamiliar words in
unison. Or so I thought.

The night we arrived at the Palermo airport, we had
learned of our lost bags and set out for our destination,

theoretically an hour from the airport, but for us, a full four hours. Had we been able to understand the charming old folk (always dressed in black and sitting in chairs by the side of the road), we would have asked directions and quite possibly have arrived before dark. I had stopped counting the times Francesca had said, "If only we had that dictionary." I kept telling her because the Sicilian dialect is different, the dictionary might not have made a difference, but I don't think she believed me. By the time we arrived at San Vito, we were both fairly ragged, and she insisted on flagging down two macho-looking motorcycle carbineri to ask directions. When they finally realized that my Sicilian-looking wife did not speak the language, the officers asked to see the hotel reservations. They glanced at the name of the hotel, puffed up their much-too-hairy chests and motioned us to follow. Although it was a memorable arrival, pulling into the hotel with a motorcycle police escort was not what I had in mind for the first night of our honeymoon.

Once in our room, I had suggested we slip into something more comfortable before remembering we had no extra clothes. Francesca rolled her eyes at me and pointed this out. We then headed out into the balmy night air to wander amongst the throngs of sweaty and perfumed Sicilian youth who streamed along the crowded promenade. At the gelato shop, we used sign language to purchase water and ice cream sandwiches, which proved to be gelato stuffed

between two pieces of bread resembling a sliced ba-
gel. After a last tasty, cool swallow of sweetness, we
slipped into one of the stores for toothbrushes and
toothpaste because Francesca once wrote a story on
dental hygiene and the evils of plaque left on one's
teeth, even for a night. While I shelled out several
euros, she studied the red and white toothpaste pack-
aging where the product was described in three lan-
guages: Italian, English, and some hieroglyphics she
didn't recognize.

"Arabic, or Greek?" she wondered aloud. As we
sauntered along the promenade, my curious wife insisted she had to stop and taste the toothpaste to see if
it was the same flavor as the American kind. I watched
her dab a small bit on her pink tongue.

"Peppermint," she declared. "Tastes the same."
Ever mindful of upholding the scientific method, I
refused to agree until I sampled her mouth by kiss-
ing her there in the center of the promenade as the
crowd parted and flowed around us. A long, juicy kiss
in the middle of the locals, who fairly dripped with
Mediterranean sensuality, did not seem out of place
on a Saturday night. After, she tucked the toothpaste
carton in her purse, she said so she would remember
my kiss, but I knew she would later try to solve the hieroglyphics mystery.

"My curious wife," I said.

"So?" she replied. She tickled me, and I laughed,
showing her my best "Prince William" smile. That was

when we both became aware of someone staring at us. Scarface and a group of boys stood about fifteen feet away, watching our every move. He pointed at me, shouted something we couldn't understand, and ran away with his friends. They blended into the late night crowd on the promenade. Francesca asked me what I thought he was saying, and didn't I wonder? Not much, and certainly not as much as she.

And now, at this blue hour with my Francesca sleeping at my side, I am content to look out the window at the palm tree tops whipping back and forth in the wind. I get up, open the door to let in a breeze. A blast of warm sirocco blows in, and voices drift up from the restaurant that lies directly underneath our balcony, below a white canvas tent roof. I hear a rustling noise from behind me. With a sheet wrapped around her, Francesca comes over to join me on the balcony. I pull her close. Together we stare out at the Tyrrhenian Sea, down at the white sandy beach, now almost deserted. Hearing a loud flapping noise, we look down to see the canvas restaurant roof below roiling in the wind. In the tarp's middle, in a low area, lies a pair of red trunks. A very familiar pair of red trunks.

"Really!" I say. "At least they were cheap." But Francesca has a plan. We both slip into our wrinkled airplane clothes and head back to the lobby to speak with Giorgia before dinner. After several minutes trying to explain what has happened, and many hand gestures, Giorgia reassures us.

"You get them back tonight when the lady with the special implement to do this arrives," she says.

Francesca and I thank her, and head to the restaurant area under the canopy that holds my trunks the wind kidnapped. We speculate about what the special implement could be, and we talk about why we ended up in a place that requires funny tools to deal with climate-induced catastrophes.

After dinner, we return for our nightly stroll along the promenade among the youthful throngs. Passing by an Indian street vendor, I am tempted to buy another pair of trunks. I am about to bargain when Francesca grabs my arm and pulls me into the human stream moving up the promenade.

"There he is," she says. Scarface is about twenty feet ahead of us, wearing a yellow tee shirt and slouching against the side of a bank along with a gang of friends. Francesca weaves her way through the crowd with an occasional, "Excusi, excusi," while I reluctantly follow.

"Do you see him?" she asks.

"Yes, he's right there, next to the ATM machine. Probably waiting to rob someone."

"He is not. Come on. Let's introduce ourselves." She tugs at my hand.

"Francesca, no," I say, trying to stop her. She attempts to pull away, but I don't let go. I hold tight to her hand, and we stand still as the stream of Sicilians pass by. She glowers at me.

"Don't you want to know what he's been saying? Don't you even care?" She yanks free, stomps away, blends into the human flow, but only for a few seconds. I cannot let her go alone. Curiosity killed the cat, and God only knows where it will take my Francesca this night.

"Excusi, excusi," I say. I push towards her and the "Banco" where I expect to find her chatting it up with the boys, or getting mugged. When I catch up, she is alone and talking to herself.

"Yerah, lefka," she chants. "Yerah, lefka."

"Yerah, lefka?"

"Yerah, lefka. Help me remember it, okay?"

"Yerah, lefka," I reply.

"Those were his exact words when he saw me."

"Did you meet him?" I ask.

"No," she sulks. "I would have if you hadn't insisted on holding me back."

"Listen, I didn't want you to get in trouble. That's all." She walks slightly in front of me, keeping enough distance to let me see she's mad, in case I hadn't noticed.

"You're so damned uncurious!" she yells, and I am glad no one else can understand. She makes my lack of curiosity sound like a federal crime.

"I promised to love, honor, and cherish—not to follow you on a wild goose chase," I say. Apparently, these are the wrong words. She does not answer, and in silence, we head back to our hotel.

When we enter the lobby, a jubilant Giorgia informs us our bags "has arrived and are in room."

"Thank you," I say. Francesca asks Giorgia if she knows the meaning of "yerah, lefka."

"Sorry, no," Giorgia answers, adding "good night."

We return to our room and open the door to the still warm night breeze and the sound of drumbeats below. I stand on our balcony, look out to see a circle of twenty or more tanned, bare-chested men pounding on drums, yelling and laughing. A group of youth gathers around them. One wears a yellow shirt. I turn and go back into our room. I do not tell her I think I have spotted Scarface for she will surely fly down to that beach and into the center of trouble.

Inside, I find her with the open suitcase looking for the Italian-English dictionary. She finds it, pulls it out, flips through the pages.

"None of them even sounds like the words he spoke," she says. I go to her, and we huddle together over the dictionary.

"It's probably the Sicilian dialect," I reassure her. She lets me nuzzle into her soft, dark hair. I trail my hand down the groove in the middle of her long, smooth back. "You know, Francesca, I am curious." I cup my hands around the gentle flair of her hips. "About some things."

"Um," she moans. And then, "I shouldn't have yelled at you in the street."

"No apologies needed," I mumble in her hair as we fall into the cool sheets. We forget about our spat and pass the dark hours moving to the rhythm of the insomniac drummers.

The next morning, I tread lightly over to the door, open the curtains, sneak onto the balcony. A scrim of clouds is high above in a cerulean sky. On the white sand below are sleeping forms. One wears a yellow shirt.

It appears that our friend and his gang have fallen asleep by last night's drum circle on the beach. I glance back at our bed, ponder waking up Francesca to tell her. Instead I watch her lips flutter with sweet breath. We are so different, she and I. She is dark and inquisitive and everything matters much to her. The opposite of my pale, and I admit, mild-mannered self. I do not know how it will all unfold in the days, months, and years before us. I do not care, I think, as I watch her sleeping deeply and peacefully, her curiosity wheels slowed down in slumber.

And then I know what I will do, what I must. I dress quietly and leave a note on the bedside table. I softly close the door behind me as I depart, head out of the hotel, into the fresh morning.

The street is mainly deserted except for the sounds of garbage trucks banging through the back alleys. When I arrive at the beach I wonder how wise it is to be here. I slow down as I walk towards the sleeping forms lying in the distance. I think of Francesca and continue on. I head for the boy in the yellow shirt. I stoop down, gently shake his shoulder.

"Excusi," I say, and stand back so as not to crowd him. His dark eyes open, then widen. I wave my hand at him, try to reassure him in sign language that I mean him no harm. And then I speak.

"Yerah, lefka?" I ask. He stands up and points at me. His buddies stir. They all scramble up in various states of dishevelment. Perplexed yet wary, they jump up to defend him, and face me. He speaks.

"Yerah, lefka, thodia," he says. His gang surrounds me.

"Yerah, lefka, thodia," they join in. I put my hands over my empty pockets, realize how foolish I am to have put myself in this position. They move in closer, surrounding me. I smell their sour breaths, hear their voices grow louder.

"Yerah, lefka, thodia, yerah, lefka, thodia," they chant together, circling me like tigers engulfing Sambo. Are these the last words I'll hear before being assaulted by a gang of twelve and thirteen-year-olds? All I can do is shout back the only thing I know they'll understand.

"Yerah, lefka, thodia!" I yell. Scarface bursts out laughing. He points at me, and all his friends snigger with him. He gives me a cocky smile, turns, and struts off followed by the others. Not quite understanding what has happened, I stand for a moment and collect myself, marvel at the solitude of the beach, the contrast between the creamy, grainy sand and the smooth, calm sea beyond. Suddenly aware of being watched, I turn around, look up. Francesca stands on the balcony wearing a sheer nightgown. She waves at me, and I wave back.

Back in our room, I reveal the last word of the phrase that has baffled her. To reward me for my investigative service, as she calls it, she kisses me. And more.

For the next two days of our honeymoon, I am her hero. We enjoy the sights, the beach, and each other. We do not see him in any of our travels, and she does not speak of him, although I know she has not forgotten. I see her eyes searching the tanned faces wherever we go. Sometimes at the beach while she thinks I am napping, I see her flip through the dictionary, trying to find the words.

Our final night in San Vito before leaving for Agrigento and the temples, we eat moussaka and drink wine at a small café on the promenade with a seaside view. We are served by a waiter, Tony, who speaks some English. He tells us he worked at his cousin's restaurant in New York for a year. Francesca is thrilled because at last she has the chance to ask someone the meaning of the mystery words that have so puzzled her.

"Yerah, lefka, thodia?" Francesca says to Tony.

"Yerah, lefka, thodia," he says. She nods. Her hands are cupped in expectation; she is a bird waiting for a worm. He shakes his head.

"Is not Italian," he says. "Is Greek." She tilts her head.

"Greek? Are you certain?"

"Yes, I part Italian, part Greek," he says. "My father leave Greece, come here, sell things at street."

"Oh, your dad was a street vendor?" asks Francesca.

"Yes, he sell rug, many year ago," Tony answers. Francesca reaches down for her purse, pulls out the red and white toothpaste box she kept as a souvenir. She hands it to Tony.

"Well, maybe you can tell me what I suspect. Is this Greek?" she asks, pointing at the hieroglyphics. Tony nods then reads the words on the box.

"Yerah, lefka, thodia," he says. "Fresh breath, strong, white teeth, no cavities." Francesca begins to laugh uncontrollably, contagiously. I tilt my head back and laugh with her. She points to my large white teeth—rabbit teeth, she calls them, and lets the words tumble out between laughs.

"Don't you see? Scarface was talking about your teeth," she says. Tears slip down her face. The sirocco whispers at my back. I think of licking the wet drops off her olive cheeks, then stop myself. I wonder if her tears would taste as salty as the sea beyond?

Italy

LAVANDERIA AUTOMATICA

She left her hotel near the Piazza Navona and walked the three blocks to the laundromat, or lavanderia automatica as the Italians called it, carrying a garbage bag full of dirty clothes. The hotel had no laundry machines, and she and her husband had run out of clean clothes. Although it was her vacation, she felt she had to find a laundromat, or so she told her husband when he said he wanted to take a second tour of the Coliseum. She had seen enough death for one trip, and one more story about the gladiators' gruesome games was one too much. So she bundled up their soiled clothes and followed her guidebook directions through a maze of narrow streets to an alley ten minutes' walk from their hotel.

Yes, they had run out of clean clothes, but the truth was that Cecilia loved going to laundromats in different cities. While others might put a museum or a restaurant on their "must see" list when they visited Paris, or Rome, where she was now, Cecilia always made the local laundromat a "must see" by at least the fourth day of any trip. She reasoned that by always washing clothes on the fourth day, she could travel lightly with only a carry-on bag. Really, though, what she had never told anyone was that she loved being in the laundromat. The soap smells, the industrious nature of people washing their laundry, the hypnotic spell she experienced while watching clothes through the dryer window as they rose up, then fell down, in perfect rhythm to the machine's thump-thump. At the laundromat, she felt at home.

She approached what seemed to be the laundromat, although there was no identifying sign outside. This one was long and narrow, tucked in an alley just down from some dark and musty cathedral she had visited the day before. After a five-hour tour of the Vatican Museum, and seeing the Sistine Chapel, she was on cultural overload.

The glass door was ajar, welcoming visitors inside. The proprietor had thoughtfully put two benches just outside the door. She scanned the room for a Coke machine and saw none. As soon as she put the clothes in, she'd look around for a Coca-Cola Lite, the slim, European version of her favorite drink. Drinking a Coke, or the bastardized version, was part of her laundromat ritual.

She walked across the worn linoleum floor in search of a change machine but saw none. A man with a bronzed face and in tight jeans noticed her and came over. The attendant. At first she had assumed he was a fellow washer but no, he was the man in charge she realized when he asked her in rudimentary English, did she need coins? Or at least that's what she thought he was saying.

"You American?" he asked.

"Yes," she said.

"Plenty dirty clothes," he said. She nodded, noticing his not unpleasant smile. A joke. She smiled back and followed him to a small desk where he had a change box. He gave her some coins in exchange for two paper bills.

At the washer she carefully loaded her clothes around the agitator which rose from the drum like an angry shaft. Who had designed these machines? A man, no doubt. No thought to how the repeated rubbing of the agitator would wear out the clothes. Looking at the machine's design, she missed her own machine back at home, a front loader with an empty and inviting drum. She was studying the instructions when the attendant sauntered over and offered to put in the correct amount of coins. She hesitated. Was he trying to scam her? Seeing her hesitation, he spoke.

"More money," he said. "I do it." He gestured toward several baskets of clothes stacked in a corner. Oh, his job was doing others' laundry, too.

"How many?" she said and held out her palm bearing the coins. He held up four fingers. She counted out four and handed them over. Although she was fairly sure she could insert them into the slot, he looked like he wanted to. It was his job. When in Rome…she was a world traveler, she knew the rules. She let him.

Once the washing machine lids were safely locked, she wandered onto the cobblestoned street to find a small mercato where she purchased a Coke Lite. She popped open the tab—took a long sip. She sighed and let her shoulders down, headed for one of the benches. As the late afternoon sun warmed her skin, and the muffled sound of the machines soothed her soul, she pulled out her journal and penned an entry.

The laundromat is a great equalizer. No class distinctions here. It all boils down to coins in a slot, which machine is available, or not. In a Paris laundromat, you can see a toothless woman washing her tattered garments, or a young mother tenderly placing tiny dresses and stuffed animals into the dryer. At the laundromat, you'll see people you won't see at your hotel or in a museum.

If you are traveling with someone else, your husband for example, by the fourth day of your journey you'll be tired of seeing the sights and each other. Going to the laundromat will give you a much needed, justifiable break. No one will want to accompany you, and you'll finally have a few moments to yourself. At the laundromat you'll enjoy perfect anonymity; no one will talk to you—

"You travel alone?" the attendant's voice interrupted her flow. She stopped writing and looked up to see him lighting a cigarette.

"No, my husband will be here soon to help me carry the clothes," she said. He looked down at her pale-as-the-moon calves protruding from black Capri pants.

"I see," he said. What did he see? She wondered. That her calves were not so slim, that her husband wasn't around, so he was free to flirt? Did this man not care if her calves were plump? Did Italian men in fact prefer a fleshier calf? The last time she was in Rome—could it really have been twenty-one years ago?—she wore shorts and wondered why the Italian men pinched her rear.What a silly girl she'd been. These capris were modest in comparison.

"Why he no carry you clothes here?" he asked. She shrugged.

He flicked his ashes onto the cobblestones, licked his lips, and went back inside. He really did have full lips. She continued writing.

—unless you are in Rome and wearing Capri pants that show your calves. You might be asked why isn't your husband carrying your laundry? You could say, "I'm strong and capable," or you might honestly answer, "I needed a break." And if you've been squeezed into a hotel room smaller than your bathroom back home, you will.

Her pen poised over the last word. She felt someone staring at her. She glanced up to see the attendant leaning against the wall, smoking a cigarette, drinking in the sight of her, a middle-aged woman writing in her journal. He cast his eyes downward as soon as she looked at him, made a loud sucking-in noise as he inhaled.

Trouble was that even if she were attracted to him, and maybe she was in an odd way, she really did want to be alone. To savor the thump-thumping of damp laundry rising up in the dryer drum, and falling down to the bottom. The towels, pants, tops and socks had no choice as they journeyed together—all caught in the pattern of rolling up, over, and falling down—a pattern dictated by being stuck inside a dryer. She found comfort in the predictability of the process, in watching garments that seemed to commit little suicides. Over and over. Those spinning bits of cloth never learned. But then what choice did they have?

She stood up and went inside to check her wash, and just in time. The cycle lights blinked off as she approached. She pulled out heavy, damp pieces, pressed them against her chest, walked over to the dryer. Before she could reach up to open the door, the attendant appeared and pulled it open. She nodded in thanks, tossed it all in except for a pair of purple and pink striped panties that tumbled to the floor. The attendant picked them up with nimble fingers and tossed them in with the rest of the load. She felt a flush pass through her.

"You need me?" he asked.

"What?" she asked. She was still thinking about those panties.

"Put in?" he asked and held out his hand. Oh, money. She dug in her pocket and pulled out some coins.

"Yes, that would be nice," she said. As he inserted the coins, she glanced down at her blouse, now translucent from the damp laundry. Instead of drawing attention to her chest, she trained her eyes on the fine brown hairs of the attendant's arm, the confident flick of his fingers as he drove the coins into the slot and pushed the button. The dryer started up. He walked away to the folding table and turned up the volume on a radio. An American song, "The Name Game," was on.

"Shirley, Shirley, Bo Burley, Shirley," the song played. The attendant snapped his fingers to the tune. "You Shirley?" he asked. She shook her head.

"Banana?" he asked. She laughed.

"Cecilia," she said.

"Cecilia, we go wait out," he said. She followed him outdoors and sat on the bench. He remained standing, lit up another cigarette. Once again she heard him inhale deeply with the sucking noise.

"Husband no come?" he asked.

"He said he would. He's on his way, I'm sure." But she really wasn't. She pulled out her journal and pretended to read.

"Cecilia, I close door when you clothes finish, when you Victoria Secret no more wet." He licked his lips but didn't look directly at her. Instead he glanced down the alley at the lowering sun.

She wasn't sure if she was flattered or frightened. He stood between her and the sun, his shadow looming over her. It was late. Where was Martin? Had he decided to take a night tour of the Coliseum? Then she remembered hearing him mumble, "If I don't get there by sundown, I'll meet you at the hotel, and we'll have a late supper in the piazza." He had said it as if it were an afterthought. The bastard had never intended to come help her carry the laundry!

"Giovanni," the attendant said. Cecilia looked up. He touched his chest with his wide hand. "Giovanni, Bo Banni, Giovanni." He smiled. The skin around his gray-green eyes was weathered, but his mouth was young, hopeful. He was probably about forty-five but looked older except for his body, that of a much younger man.

He motioned for her to go inside. She rose and walked through the doorway toward the spinning dryer. He followed her, closing the door behind. She heard the click of the door lock. The room was suddenly dim. He had switched off the lights.

Standing in front of the dryer, she watched her clothes spin round and round through the big glass window. She felt the warmth of him near her.

"Cecilia," he said. He traced his fingertips up her bare arm, caressed her delicate cheekbone, and put his thumb under her chin.

She let him turn her head towards his face. He leaned in to kiss her, and she did not stop him. She felt his full lips press against hers, felt his fingertips brush over her damp chest, trail down her belly to her rounded hips. His hands gripped her rump. He lifted her onto the counter situated below the soap dispenser.

She glimpsed at the dryer, saw the tangled clothes rise to the top, then fall down. Over and over. A forward movement that could not be stopped. Little suicides.

Sicily

ERICE

Not only were the fields empty, they were burning. Fires burned in long, glowing arcs making their way across the gleaned fields of the Sicilian countryside. It was early September, still torrid, and the harvest was over, yet the local farmers thought it necessary to set the remaining stubble on fire. Why, Kate wondered, were they doing this, and if they had a reason, why could they not wait until it cooled down some? Why add more heat to the inferno now blasting through the windows of the rented Renault? If her son, Ned, were with her, Kate thought, they would joke about the logic of setting fires in all this heat. "Like setting a fire—" she would say.

"In hell," he would interrupt, finishing her sentence for her as he always did. They would laugh together.

"Pardon?" Carter asked. Kate glanced over at her gentle and serious husband, his firm grip on the steering wheel, his focus on the narrow road. She realized she must have spoken aloud.

"Nothing," she said, carefully hoarding her thoughts of their son for herself. She did not want to share the fact with Carter that she had in fact been mired down in thoughts of Ned during the entire eighteen-hour journey since they left Los Angeles. She had been looking forward to this trip for some time, her own reward for having gotten Ned off to college three weeks earlier. All through the summer, she and Carter had laughed and joked as they talked about the days to come, the freedom to travel together to his scientific conferences. But now she had arrived at this place in her life she had dreamed of for so long, she was surprised to find her mind wandering back to her son. An oasis in her mind for so many years, freedom had turned out to be a bitter sip of espresso.

For years, she had anticipated the day her son would be at college, and her calendar would be filled with blank days, freeing her to do her art. Over the summer, she had been hired to paint the illustrations for a children's book. Although her deadline wasn't until December, and she had begun drawing in July, she bogged down by early August when she started packing Ned for college. Since his departure in mid-August, she had lived through twenty-one blank days and had only a white canvas to show for it.

That something was amiss was obvious to her husband, Carter, who had noticed her subdued manner.

In his mind, he assigned it a name: the dark phase. Identifying a problem was the first step in solving it, but in this case, he had no clue how. He didn't want to inquire if perhaps he had done something wrong. Over the last twenty years of marriage, he had learned it was best to let her moods play out. Besides, with such an important presentation one day off, it was best not to risk causing an uncontrolled chain reaction of female emotions that might derail his concentration. Already he had inadvertently set her off just before their departure when she insisted on upgrading their cell phones to make international calls. Carter gently reminded her of what they had learned at their son's college orientation: best not to call more than once a week. They would only be in Sicily for seven days. Kate had snapped at him, saying how absurd to think those professional home wreckers knew her son better than she. Carter knew she was referring to the orientation team who had lectured the parents at a small Massachusetts college for students with learning disabilities that Ned now attended. There, the professionals would pick up the day-to-day work of tutoring their son that Kate had shouldered for the last twelve years.

Carter said they both deserved to celebrate their graduation from the day-to-day rigors of child rearing, although to be truthful, most of the work had fallen on her while he developed software and made presentations at conferences around the world. After he attended the Interplanetary Disaster Conference, they planned to travel for another few days before heading back home to Los Angeles. He was looking forward to taking his wife with him, and while he had told no one, certainly not Kate, he was glad to have her all to himself for a change, instead of having to share her with their son.

For her, it was the first time in Sicily, although he had traveled alone once before to their destination, Erice, a small and isolated medieval town high above the sea on the island's western side. On a clear day, one could see all the way to Cape Bon, Tunisia, Carter had told Kate. By the time they arrived in late afternoon, mist had shrouded the gray stone buildings and silent cobblestone streets, and it was all they could do to find their hotel on Via Vittorio Emanuele.

They retreated to a smallish room that was saved by the door that opened onto a courtyard filled with a palette of jasmine, roses, and fuchsia. While Kate unpacked her things, Carter opened the door, letting in a heady scent that reminded him of the courtyard of their first apartment two decades before. There, the nectar of the flowers mingled with the sweetness of their lovemaking. He let his gaze move from the myriad colors of the courtyard to the violin-like curve where her waist flowed into her hip. He took a step toward her, then hesitated. "Why don't you take that chair out on the porch and enjoy the flowers?" he asked.

To Kate, his voice sounded overly considerate, patronizing. She turned away from her suitcase, towards her husband. "Maybe later," she answered pleasantly,

instead of screaming what she was thinking: stop treat-
ing me like your grandmother! For a moment, she let
herself study the pale wisp of sandy hair that fell so
carelessly, so endearingly, over his left eye and thought
of brushing it away with her finger. In that tender second she hesitated, she saw not only her husband, but
her son: the same high forehead, the same pale hair.
And so instead of moving toward the father of her
child, she moved away from him, toward the pair of
sturdy walking shoes she had placed under the wood
dresser. She always took along her comfortable shoes
and her lint pick-up stick when she traveled. Some
things you can't control, but some things you can, she
reasoned.

Carter admired her slender ankles as she tied the
thick laces into neat bows.

She thought about the way Carter had been treat-
ing her, knew he must see her as she really was. Perhaps
she had suddenly accelerated into old age and simply
was unaware of it, although her husband had noticed.
Still, forty-five didn't seem that old, unless, of course,
one was living in medieval times. Were it then, she
would most likely be dead, or almost.

"Seven?" a voice brought her from the Middle Ages
into the present. It was Carter.

"Yes, seven will be good," she said, "then we can get
to bed early." There, she had done it again. Sensible
shoes, early bed. What was next? Warm milk on the
nightstand?

Carter waved a cheery goodbye and departed for conference check-in. Men always seemed so happy when they left to attend to business. She wondered if Ned was at this very moment attending to his studies, and was he happy? She wanted to call him, but Carter kept reminding her of what they had heard had at orientation: Let them adjust. But Ned would want to know they had arrived safely, even if Carter preferred to listen to the cold-hearted professionals, the weaning crew. Feeling a bit like a thief, she unzipped Carter's duffle bag, tucked the international cell phone into her pocket, and walked out the door.

While her husband pondered catastrophes of an inner-galactic nature, she tried to untangle her own unraveling universe as she walked the streets of the quiet, stone city. After Ned was born, while he was napping one afternoon, she had talked to her own mother about the toll of creating another being. Kate explained that the pregnancy and birth of her son had left her with a diminished soul. She felt as though a piece of her soul had actually broken off and planted itself in her infant son, leaving Kate with less of herself. Kate's mother had winced at her daughter's description, and quickly tried to make everything better by stating that was why God had given Kate such a large soul. And besides, her son would enrich her life. She would soon forget about this soul nonsense. And her mother had been right. Kate had quickly come to love her son more than anything else. And although she did not realize it, at some point, her passion for her grandest creative effort, her son, had overtaken her passion for art. But her mother had never warned Kate about what would happen when the child grew up. She had not shared the truth about the child moving out, leaving behind the mother's diminished soul, emptied of all its air and light. As Kate thought of her present soul, she visualized a green hull, its smooth, concave walls, emptied of peas. The hulls were cast aside, thrown away. Pea-less, they were purposeless.

She thought of all this as she wandered the cobblestone streets and twisting alleys looking for an open space and a cell phone signal. The old town was laid out in a triangle, which made getting lost an almost certainty. Carter had warned her of this, so she was careful to note landmarks, a store here, a piazza there, as she traversed the uneven ground. For the most part, the streets were rather deserted except for the occasional pair of badge-wearing conference participants lost in scientific conversation. Perhaps the usual residents were tucked into their stone homes behind the courtyard entrances visible from the narrow streets. The brochure Carter had picked up for her near the main piazza informed her there were 250 of these courtyards and that the "diligent or curious tourist" would "feel a joyful emotion of a vision" opening a door to enter. Sneaking into someone's private courtyard was something she and Ned might have attempted, but her son was not there at that moment. On her own, she felt neither diligent, nor curious. When had she lost her sense of adventure?

Giving in to the new, apparently more subdued version of herself, she stopped at an overpriced restaurant for a cup of tea. Judging by the surly expression on the waiter's face, it was too late for lunch and too early for dinner. She sat by a huge, unlit fireplace topped off by a wide mantle covered with dozens of physics books laid out for the benefit of visiting scientists, who were frequent, Carter had told her. She eyed the pastries placed by the waiter under the nose of the book-reading, badge-wearing scientist sitting a few tables away and ordered one for herself. She ate the dry yet filling almond pastry while reading about the temple the ancient city of Erice, or Eryx, had built for Aphrodite. The ruins were now on a cliff overlooking the sea. A clear place where her phone might work. She paid the check, and for the good of womankind in general, left a large tip in order to dispel any notions the waiter might have about female generosity.

She headed east along Viale Conte Pepoli to the Castello di Venere, a twelfth century castle resting on the former site of an ancient temple built to honor Aphrodite. Old blended with new in the imposing walls which incorporated fragments from the ancient temple along with the more recent, twelfth century Castle of Venus. Kate found herself drawn to the courtyard area where pagan ceremonies were said to have taken place. Surrounded by crumbling, stone walls of mixed ages, layers of time, she contemplated the empty, weed-filled space, all that was left of the once great goddess. Even goddesses can be reduced to ruins, she thought wryly.

She moved towards a stone archway that served as a portal to a view meant for deity. But Kate, so painfully mortal, saw only portions of the cyan sea through the moving mists. She pulled out the cell phone, pushed the "on" button. There was only one bar, meaning no signal. She tried anyway but got a quick series of tones that meant the dratted thing wouldn't work. She switched it off, looked out again toward the view meant for gods, now mostly obscured by the fog. On a good day, perhaps tomorrow, the view would be better. Then again, maybe not.

As she wandered back through the mostly empty streets, she passed several emaciated dogs lying in the street, their ribs flayed out against the ancient cobblestones. There, oblivious to the town's layered history, the dogs soaked up the remaining warmth given off by the uneven stones. Ned would have loved this sight, Kate thought, snapping a picture. When she reached him, she would tell him.

It was getting late, so using the landmarks she'd noticed, Kate found her way back to the hotel to meet up with Carter. While they dressed for dinner, he told her he had run into an old acquaintance, an amiable Italian physics professor who would introduce him before he gave his "Automated Near-Earth Object

Tracking and Classification" presentation. The professor's wife, who spoke fluent English, was going sightseeing the next day and had asked if perhaps Carter's wife might want to join her.

"I've got something else planned," she answered. She didn't really, unless you counted wandering Erice's twisted alleys looking for a place the phone would work, absorbing the stone city's gray silence that seemed to match her mood. She just didn't like Carter trying to plan her schedule for her.

At the trattoria, they were seated next to two German scientists who appeared to intensely debate some theory or another. Kate talked about her afternoon and told Carter about the now-decaying temple site which promised to have a remarkable view, once the sun appeared.

"After the conference, I'd like to see it," he said. "I've got to review my notes tomorrow morning."

"Yes, I know," she said. All at once, a couple showed up to occupy the vacant seats next to them. The man's clothes were slightly rumpled, and the woman wore the flush of recent lovemaking. Carter introduced him as the Italian professor he had mentioned earlier. The professor said to please call him Paolo and introduced his wife as Giovanna. They turned to their menus, and Kate watched the intense, dark, and apparently ravenous, much too young wife order in rapid-fire Italian. The waiter brought out Kate and Carter's secondi course, grilled shrimp that had gotten cold. Carter's Italian was not as good as he'd thought, and he'd ordered the special, not realizing it was shrimp. Kate had always hated the pinkish crustaceans curled in fetal positions. Dead babies is what Ned called them. She smiled at the thought of him and picked at her plate.

Carter noticed her expression and was encouraged.

"I'm sorry. They're not so bad, really, are they?" he asked.

"Mine seem to be behaving," she said.

"Funny you," he answered, glad to see her abstract, albeit corny, sense of humor surface. "You know you could come to the conference, if you like. You might find it fascinating."

"No more than this fortress of a town," she answered.

"Then you like it?" he asked. Before Kate had a chance to answer, the young wife spoke.

"Excuse me. I hope you will forgive me for interrupting. I have observed that Erice, it is a man's town. These hard and strong walls, these fortifications. All very male. Don't you agree?"

"Yes. So much stone," Kate said, not adding that the stone seemed to ruin cell phone signals.

"Perhaps tomorrow you will let me show you the temples in Agrigento," Giovanna said, reaching over and touching Carter's arm. "Will you let me take your wife tomorrow on the natives' tour?"

Carter looked at Kate. "It's up to my lovely wife."

Giovanna laughed and grabbed her husband's hands.

"You see, you are not the only charming man here," she spoke to her husband in a low growl, then turned back to Kate. "I am leaving at eight—it's more than a hundred kilometers." Giovanna said. "If you don't want to come, I may be forced to go alone to enjoy the Valley of the Temples."

By the time the waiter brought the espresso and amoretti, Kate knew she would say yes. Giovanna had been educated in Milan and spoke perfect English, making her the ideal tour guide for a woman who was feeling most unadventurous. Besides, there was a possibility the cell phone would work better away from the medieval city's stone walls.

The next morning Kate arose at seven and dressed purposefully. Carter watched her brush her long, chestnut hair. He saw as she slipped her cream-colored linen shift over her bare shoulders, and already he missed her. Yet he knew this had been a good idea when he saw her studying the map last night to see where she was headed.

"Don't forget your hat and sunscreen," Carter reminded her. "The sun can be brutal."

"Especially at my age," she said, placing a white, wide-brimmed cotton hat on her head.

He hadn't thought that at all, but didn't reply. Perhaps she was joking? Her skin was as soft as a peach, and he loved to touch it, although of late, he hadn't had much of an opportunity. He had theorized that once their son left, they would become more amorous, more spontaneous. It hadn't happened. As Kate walked out the door, they brushed lips.

Kate and Giovanna headed out of Erice's forested hills, down to the coastal town of Trapani, and onto the autostrade. There, the Sicilian drivers had no sense of fear, and Giovanna, a native of Palermo, was no exception. Kate's fingers clung to the edges of her leather seat as Giovanna pushed the Fiat past another car, gaining a mere car length.

"Don't worry," Giovanna assured Kate. "Paolo says I drive as well as I make love." Kate watched her stroke through the gears and figured it must be true. She then relaxed in her seat to take in the scenery.

They pushed through the interior, dotted with olive and almond trees, scrub brush and oleanders and more hot, dry towns than Kate had ever seen in California. They passed the harvested and burned fields she had seen on the way in, finally arriving at the coastal route in the town of Sciacca. From then on, Kate caught occasional peeks of the sea through the olcander bushes as they headed east.

Except for the wild driving, Giovanna was pleasant to be with and an informed tour guide. She had spent time in the Sicilian countryside with her grandmother, who was born in Cattolica, near Agrigento. She had studied English, French, and literature in college and had an answer for every question. Ned would have loved her. When they stopped at a gas station for fuel, Kate tried again to dial Ned on the cell phone but was unsuccessful. The thing simply wasn't working at this location. Perhaps when they reached Agrigento...

Back on the road, when Giovanna asked if she was trying to call her lover, Kate laughed and explained it was her son. Giovanna wanted to hear all about him, so Kate lovingly described Ned for the next half hour. She talked about his shy smile, his fine, blonde hair, his gangly basketball player body, and his clumsy streak. She explained his attention deficit disorder to Giovanna, who asked, "like the absent-minded professor?" Yes, Kate said, and told her how his condition affected more than his school work, how one morning before school he had climbed into Kate's car wearing no shoes. He simply forgot to put them on.

"You must miss him," Giovanna said. and Kate hesitated for a moment, then answered.

"I do," she said, admitting aloud for the first time how she felt. Why was it so easy to say to an almost stranger what she could not easily tell her own husband?

"In my country, after the children finish college, they often move back home until they marry," Giovanna explained.

"Maybe I should move to Italy," Kate said.

"You would not have to give your son up, ever. And you would be doing his laundry when you were ninety-five." They were still laughing when they arrived at the outskirts of Agrigento.

There, they were greeted by a juxtaposition of ugly, tall modern buildings that gave the city an industrial look, not what Kate expected. Giovanna had told her how the Greek poet, Pindar, described the city, Akragas, as the most beautiful city of mortals. Kate could not see it and said so. Giovanna explained that the modern city, built on a higher ridge, was more visible, but that the ancient city, built in 581 B.C. on a lower ridge, was the place Pindar meant. They exited the highway and wound their way through the city, finally reaching the Valle de Templi area. Giovanna announced it was time for lunch, and they stopped at the Hotel Villa Athena. With a view of the stately temples in the distance, the two women ate crispy rice balls filled with cheese, cooked escarole with olive oil, and pieces of hard, crusty bread. Giovanna ordered their drinks, Tintorettos, or glasses of sparkling wine and pomegranate juice, served in wine glasses. She made a toast.

"To Demeter and Persephone and their island," she said, as their glasses clinked. Giovanna told her that in ancient times, the Sicilians believed Demeter brought corn to the island. She was known as the goddess who was responsible for the various crops and especially grain. Later, she had forbidden the crops to grow when her daughter, Persephone, was kidnapped by Hades and taken to the underworld. He agreed to let her return to Demeter but tricked her into eating some pomegranate seeds, meaning she had to return for six months of the year.

Kate had heard the story before, and when they ordered two more of the Tintorettos, she made her own toast. "To the return of Persephone," she said. Soon the sirocco picked up, blowing its hot breath on Kate's tender face. They got up to leave. When Kate stood, the strap of her handbag slipped off her shoulder causing her purse to brush against the table and tip over the remaining half-glass of Tintoretto. Red-purple liquid splashed down the front hem of her ivory dress. Using a damp napkin, Giovanna tried to help her clean off the stains, but Kate was so hot, she simply wanted to leave, perhaps find a cool place indoors. Instead, Giovanna insisted on taking her to the temples before dark.

Thus, Kate found herself following her energetic young tour guide up a dusty road in the arid afternoon. She listened as Giovanna described the temples of Herakles, Concord, and Hera. Two of the temples were in various stages of decay, some missing columns, but the Templio della Concordia was preserved perfectly. Giovanna kept trying to get Kate interested in the columns while Kate was more interested in tombs and catacombs visible from the dusty lane. Kate asked if they could go there.

"These are closed," Giovanna answered, sitting down on a low wall by an olive tree to take a swig of water from the plastic bottle they had purchased at one of the snack and souvenir stands ringing the Valley of the Temples. Kate sat down next to her, and together they took in the view to the sea.

Giovanna explained how the temples served as a deterrent to potential invaders. "Back in these times, people believed the gods lived inside the temples. The more temples they erected, the more gods were in residence. People passing by on the sea saw the temples and were intimidated and hopefully did not invade the city. That's why they are built high up, quite visible to people passing by in boats on the sea."

The words that Kate heard were "high up," so when a couple of white-haired ladies stopped to ask Giovanna for directions to the museum, she pulled out the cell phone. She keyed in Ned's number and heard a faint ring. The call went through, and Kate heard her son's sweet voice answer. Light and air and excitement rushed into her.

"Ned? It's Mom. I had to call you. I'm standing in the middle of these ancient temples that were built five hundred years before Christ was born. And oh, there were fires all over the fields, even though it's hotter than, well, hell. And there were these emaciated dogs lying around the cobblestone streets. I wish you were here." She paused for a second to give him a chance to answer.

"Mom?" he said.

"Yes?"

"We're studying for a math quiz.".

"We?"

"Me and my tutor," he said.

And then Kate heard a female voice in the background.

"My tutor and I," the voice corrected. Laughter followed, Ned and the tutor's.

"I'm too busy to talk right now, Mom," Ned said. "Can you call me later?"

Kate started to explain about the lack of phone service in Sicily when the line went dead. Her body slumped down, and she felt the hard stones of the wall against her underside, felt more ancient than the ruins around her. Giovanna took one look at her and grabbed her by the hand.

"It's too hot up here for you at this moment. Come."

Kate was not so much hot as she was numb. She stood up, let herself be led by the younger woman. Taking a shortcut, they climbed over a wall near the side of the temple and moved through a field to a road and past another temple, finally reaching a main road. They walked in silence, which was fine with Kate. She couldn't get over the fact that Ned did not really want to talk with her. Those cold-hearted professional weaners had succeeded in alienating her son.

They continued past a cemetery and followed an unpaved road to a church perched on the edge of a cliff. A Norman church, San Biago, was built in the

twelfth century and featured side walls integrated
with the foundation and part of the walls of the older Temple of Demeter and Persephone, built in the
fourth century B.C., Giovanna told her. Kate was content to stand in front of the church, staring at the mingled walls of old and older. It was easier to contemplate
these stone layers of time than to think about the pain
she felt when her son hung up on her. She would have
stood there until dark had Giovanna not touched her
arm, steered her towards the rear of the church.

"It's what is below that is important," Giovanna
said. "My grandmother showed me this place." Behind
the old church was a gate which Giovanna expected to
find locked, but it was not. She hurried Kate through
the gate. "Quickly," she said, leading Kate down a steep
stairway. "If he sees us, the farmer who watches out for
this place will make us leave. It is officially closed from
the landslides."

They arrived at a quiet, cool place shaded by pine
trees, stood in the ruins of an even earlier time, the
Sanctuario Rupestre di Demetra, or rock Sanctuary of
Demeter. Giovanna explained that the sanctuary was
built in the fifth century B.C., possibly earlier. They
stood inside a series of low walls and stared at three
openings in the cliff. Although the openings were gated off, Giovanna said she had heard there were tunnels leading to squared or rounded rooms. Some said
the rooms had cisterns used by worshipers. One of the
tunnels was supposed to have an aqueduct that carried

water from a spring deep in the hillside, but there was not even a trickle in sight. Giovanna thought she heard a noise coming from above the stairs.

Giovanna whispered,"That is the farmer, I am afraid. I'll stall him with a tip. You come up as soon as you've looked around." And then she left Kate alone.

Tucking her slim ankles under her body, Kate settled back on one of the sanctuary's low walls and imagined the worshipers of Demeter at this very spot 2,500 year ago. She stared at the gated tunnels, looking for a trickle of water that had flowed from a spring deep in the earth. She saw none. She felt so alone in this quiet, eerie place where the earth itself had wept. She thought of Demeter and her rage and sorrow at the loss of her child. And then Kate let herself travel through her own layers, through the numbness, past the rage and sorrow, to her center. Until now, she had not allowed herself to acknowledge this feeling that had presented itself the day they dropped Ned off at college. She had ignored the feeling, hoping it would go away. It had not.

So it was there, at the place where the ancients had worshiped Demeter, Kate finally felt the emptiness in her core, acknowledged her own bleak winter, a place where Hades had stolen Persephone away. At that moment, in the ancient sanctuary where the goddess and her daughter were once worshiped, she understood why Demeter had forbidden the crops to grow. The goddess of grain needed to share her rage and sorrow with the world. Not even an immortal could face losing a child alone.

For several minutes, Kate sat among the ruins, at peace with the cold season within. Finally, as the setting sun cast long shadows along the low-slung walls of the sanctuary, she stood up to leave the most ancient of ruins. Slowly she ascended the stairs and did not look back.

Giovanna was at the top smoking a cigarette, watching the last rays of the sun play against the Valley of the Temples. The two women did not talk as they headed back toward the temples on the hill high above the sea. Kate did not have to tell her what had happened. Giovanna knew the Sanctuario to be a healing place; her grandmother had told her. They headed back the way they had come, walked past the Temple of Concordia standing bold and elegant in the floodlight with its many Doric columns. Kate suddenly wished she could draw the temple and its perfect columns, but she could not. Her sketchbook was back at the hotel room in Erice, and so was her husband.

When she returned there, she would tell Carter all she had felt for the past three weeks. She would explain how Ned's leaving had made her inexplicably angry with Carter, the same way she felt during her labor. Carter had given her the gift of Ned, the son she loved more than anything. The gift had come with much pain—in childbirth and upon her son's departure. And as irrational as it sounded, even to Kate, she both loved and was infuriated with Carter for this bittersweet gift. She did not know how she could explain the way she felt. She would try.

When Kate climbed into the car, she looked down at the red-purple stain on her hem and knew what she would do tomorrow while Carter was at the conference. Sitting at the table in the colorful, flowered courtyard next to their room, she would draw some sketches for the still life she planned to paint when they got back home to California. She would think about the colors to use, the deep pink-red tones for the leathery skin, the lighter pink-white for the plump seeds, the pale ivory tones for the membrane. She would paint a pomegranate split wide open. She would place the pomegranate painting on her studio wall to remind her of the sweet and tart juice she had tasted. And when Ned came home to visit, she would show him the painting. Before he had a chance to ask, she would reveal to him how many seeds it had, 840. He would say, "But did you count?" And they would laugh.

ACKNOWLEDGMENTS

A special thank you to my writer friends Kathe Traynham and Anne Turley for meticulously reading my manuscript, to Amber Lanier Nagle for designing my cover, and to my usual cheerleaders, my family, friends, my Chattarosa writing group sisters, and especially to all my reader friends who kept asking for the next book.

Many thanks also to the editors who had faith in my work, especially Alicia Clavell of *Southern Women's Review,* for publishing four of my stories. I am grateful to the Pirates Alley Faulkner Society for honoring one of my stories as finalist ("Erice") and another as semi-finalist ("Leaving Bruges") in their short story competition. And to family and friends who listened as I kept talking about these stories, thank you for your patience and encouragement.

The following short stories that appear in this anthology were originally published elsewhere as listed below.

"Under Milkweed Leaves" *Southern Women's Review*, Spring 2010, Volume 2, Library of Congress ISSN # 1947-976X

"Backyard Messages" *Southern Women's Review*, Summer/Fall 2010, Volume 3, Library of Congress ISSN # 1947-976X

"Hiatus" *Blue Crow Magazine*, April 2010, Issue I, The Blue Crow Press, Sydney, Australia

"Moon Ride, Summer, 1959" *A Tapestry of Voices*, 2011, ISBN: 0-9643178-7-1

"Rotten Apples" *Southern Women's Review*, January 2013, Library of Congress ISSN # 1947-976X

"Journey to Yanu" *Southern Women's Review*, January 2014, Library of Congress ISSN # 1947-976X

"Aunt Trish's Wedding Gift"*Broken Petals* (an Appalachian-inspired short story collection), 2014, JCP, Inc. ISBN 10:1939289327